A Thorn in the Bush

A Thorn in the Bush

Frank Herbert

WordFire Press
Colorado Springs, Colorado

ISBN: 978-1-61475-283-7

Cover design by Kevin J. Anderson

Art Director Kevin J. Anderson

Cover artwork images by Dollar Photo Club

Book Design by RuneWright, LLC
www.RuneWright.com

Published by
WordFire Press, an imprint of
WordFire, Inc.
PO Box 1840
Monument CO 80132

Kevin J. Anderson & Rebecca Moesta, Publishers

WordFire Press Trade Paperback Edition November 2014
Printed in the USA
wordfirepress.com

Chapter 1

But what if the young man is innocent?" asked Don Jaime. He spoke in Spanish with a lisping Castilian accent, an affectation that marked him as a man of some daring among Mexican politicians.

"Innocent!" Mrs. Ross put all the scorn of her seventy-one years into the word. "I tell you he is precisely like the other one!" Her Spanish lashed at him, full of overtones from countless kitchen maids and with hardly a trace remaining of her native English.

"But … but …" Don Jaime sputtered at her as only the mayor of a small town can sputter at a rich land owner and valued confidante. "You cannot come here and ask me to imprison a tourist simply because he reminds you of someone out of your past! Please? You cannot." His shoulders hunched in a Latin shrug. "Emma, my dearest friend, we must remember that times change."

"But young men don't!"

They sat in Don Jaime's upstairs parlor, a plaster and blue tile room of austere furnishings. It looked out on Mexico's Lake Chapala from the waterfront of San Juan. Afternoon sunlight, reduced to narrow ribbons by venetian blinds, wove a tapestry of glowing yellow across the room.

An immense black upholstered chair enfolded Mrs. Ross, dwarfed her. She had presented this chair to Don Jaime on his Saint's Day ten years ago because she could not endure sitting in any of his other furniture. Every other chair in the house presented unexpected corners, painful edges and sloping planes that kept you ever on the alert against being slid off onto the floor. She was convinced that none of these pieces had been designed for human beings.

Mrs. Ross wore a blue silk dress and a small blue-feathered hat over her grey hair. She looked like a shriveled dowager duchess: sharp-eyed and slightly sunburned so that the effect was a little horsey. Her face presented balanced planes that still revealed some of the beauty that age had covered.

Don Jaime held himself severely upright in a high-backed teak throne. He was a lean figure in a black business suit of European cut. His face—long, narrow and with pinched-in cheeks—looked like the face of the crucified Jesus that hung in San Juan's church. Although two years older than Mrs. Ross, he still retained the glossy charcoal hair of his youth.

On this afternoon there had been the long, slow ritual conversation: the inquiries about health, about mutual friends, the state of the weather, of the crops (both agricultural and tourist), and a discussion of a recent fishing tragedy at Solas farther down the lake in which a father and son had drowned. The son had been known to Serena, Mrs. Ross's current maid of all work.

During all their talk there had been persistent mouse-like sounds in a nearby room: one of Don Jaime's serving girls making work there to eavesdrop.

But now Mrs. Ross was down to the object of her visit. "I know this young man's type," she said.

"What do you *really* know about him?" asked Don Jaime.

Mrs. Ross's nose twitched in irritation. "His full name is Francis Andrew Hoblitt," she said. "He comes from St. Louis. He is twenty-eight, unmarried, speaks little Spanish ... and that poorly. I'm certain you've seen him around: a blond young man, always frowning."

"And always carrying the drawing pad." With two motions of his hands Don Jaime hung the squared-off pad shape in the air between them.

"The same. He lives in that little guest house that the Friesmans rent out. He drinks too much. He throws things ... and he doesn't like the new tax on foreign artists. He said vile things to the tax collector."

She did not add that Hoblitt, while in wine, had pinched Lolita Veras on the bottom. Hoblitt was altogether the kind of tourist who made Mrs. Ross ashamed of her countrymen.

Don Jaime nodded, averted his eyes. He had been a widower for thirty-six years, and his manner betrayed a certain watchful caution with women (although he had courted Mrs. Ross when she first arrived in San Juan in 1937).

The detailed information about Hoblitt did not surprise Don Jaime. Through her many tenants and employees, Mrs. Ross ran a first class spy system— almost as good as Don Jaime's own. And he knew that an absolute requirement for anyone working in Mrs. Ross's immediate household was the ability to relay every bit of gossip heard in the market square. Serena, the current maid, shone above all others in this capacity—a two-legged recording device who chattered endlessly at her work, telling everything she saw or heard, spicing it all with local superstitions.

"Do you think this Hoblitt is a good painter?" ventured Don Jaime.

Mrs. Ross dismissed Francis Hoblitt's work with one word: "Modern!"

Don Jaime scowled, thinking now about St. Louis, a name he had just heard in connection with Hoblitt. Don Jaime knew that St. Louis was a place name in América del Norte, very likely a large city. His knowledge of geography went little beyond awareness that Mexico City (called simply "Mexico" in the local idiom) lay somewhere vaguely eastward—not as far as the Gulf, but nonetheless a boring trip in his twelve-year-old chauffeur-driven Buick. He knew that Guadalajara lay northward up the superhighway, and that the Pacific Ocean billowed endlessly off in the west. América del Norte—that bottomless source of rich tourists—remained a geography book picture: a green, yellow, brown and pink blob occupying an immense frozen area north of the Rio Grande—which was a Mexican river.

Perhaps it is evil to come from St. Louis, thought Don Jaime. *A breeding ground of gangsters, possibly.*

He said: "You know St. Louis?"

"I've never been there."

Mrs. Ross resigned herself to a few moments of diversionary questioning, but she resolved not to be put off. *This business of Hoblitt and Paulita Romera could become tragic,* she told herself.

Don Jaime pursed his lips. "St. Louis, then, is not near to Fairbanks?" Don Jaime had been told the fiction that Mrs. Ross came from Fairbanks, Alaska, a locale he had hopelessly misplaced. He thought of Alaska as being somewhere eastward, fronting on the Atlantic Ocean, and close by the capital of América del Norte, which was a city called New York.

"It's at least three thousand miles from Fairbanks!" snapped Mrs. Ross.

Three thousand miles! An incomprehensible distance having something to do with kilometers. Don Jaime put it out of his mind.

"Perhaps it would serve if I detailed Beto to keep watch on this Señor Hoblitt," said Don Jaime. By Beto he meant his nephew, Roberto García y Machado, a mustachioed braggart and police chief of San Juan.

Mrs. Ross had never reconciled herself to Mexican political nepotism. She scowled. "You know very well, Jaime, that Beto would be off drunk somewhere when anything serious happened, and he would show up later full of stupid excuses. This is much too critical for Beto."

"But what do you expect me to do?"

"Trump up some charge against Señor Hoblitt, throw him in jail and have him deported. It's really very simple."

"Very simple!" Don Jaime threw up his hands.

"If you wish me to handle this myself, I shall!"

"Oh, no! No ... no ..." Don Jaime, instantly sobered, shook his head.

The last tourist that Emma Ross had handled herself had landed in the Guadalajara hospital, the innocent victim of a street riot, it was said, although it had been dark at the time and the only witnesses were a dozen or so tenant farmers from Mrs. Ross's lands. There had followed a sharply worded note to Don Jaime from Don Tomás Norillega, minister in charge at the Dirección General de Turismo in Mexico City. The note's substance had been: "See that such things are not repeated.

They frighten away the tourists!"

"No," said Don Jaime. "We will work out something."

"I'm sure you will."

Don Jaime turned to look out at the lake through the slatted blinds. The sun's reflection lay like a molten copper puddle on the surface of the water. He squinted. A fly buzzed his head, evaded the warding hand to alight on the glossy black hair.

It was a tragic thing, he thought. In spite of the fact that he felt he knew the *real* situation with this Hoblitt, Don Jaime's Latin heart ached with the story Mrs. Ross had told.

For her part, Mrs. Ross was reviewing the same story, wondering if she had left out some fact more apt to stir Don Jaime to action. She felt supremely sure of herself in this matter: *Urgent action is required!*

CHAPTER 2

It had begun two days ago—on Tuesday morning. The day had started (as most San Juan days did) with a stridency of church bells. A Protestant herself, Mrs. Ross frowned on this early morning clanging as a sort of pagan rite, especially when it was mixed with firecrackers. The crackers were an Indian custom, exploded to help a baby's soul to heaven. Sure enough, staccato explosions cut across the morning sounds. Another baby had died in the night.

Mrs. Ross sniffed, sat up in her bed.

Mingled odors of scorched chili peppers, charcoal, bottled gas, and coffee wafted upward to her second-floor bedroom from the kitchen. She heard a sizzle of frying—Serena with the two breakfast eggs. Presently,

Serena would appear with a tray: the eggs, buttered toast, fresh orange juice, and coffee. Like much of Mrs. Ross's life, it was an unvarying ritual.

A burro brayed on the waterfront a block away. Answering yodels echoed from farther down the lake.

Mrs. Ross swung her skinny legs out of the bed into the patch of sunshine on the Mitla serape she used as a rug. She was entirely nude, a habit adopted during her first week in San Juan. Sunshine poured onto her bony knees like a warm, golden liquid. This first feeling of the morning sun on her body always made Mrs. Ross think of the old days in Alaska—icy winds, blowing snow. It gave her a sense of accomplishment to feel the sun.

So to work, she thought.

By eight-thirty, she had breakfasted, bathed, settled the usual petitions from some of her tenants, checked the account books, and sent Serena off to market for the day's food and gossip. The morning ritual brought her now to the red-draped French doors that opened onto her balcony. She carried a hammered brass watering can, a gift from Don Jaime. It sloshed as she put it down.

Outside, growing in oblong pottery boxes along the rail, a green riot of herbs and spices perfumed the air. Their aroma penetrated the gap where the French doors did not quite meet. Mrs. Ross swung the doors open, inhaled, stretched.

The hot Mexican sun made her plants thrive so much better than they had in Alaska, she thought. But the parsley and chives drooped if they missed only one watering.

A Mexican bumblebee the size of a walnut buzzed the planters, sped off toward the *copa de oro* vine growing up the corner of the balcony.

Mrs. Ross looked down through the open work of the balcony rail, saw Paulita Romera—as always at this hour—sitting at the ground floor window of the house across the cobblestone street. Paulita held a fabric frame, sewing at *punto de cruz*—the tiny cross-stitches—working them into a floral pattern. Sometimes she knitted or tatted or crocheted intricate Mexican lace.

An exquisite young woman, thought Mrs. Ross: *more beautiful than any hundred-dollar-a-night girl I've ever seen.*

Paulita's ebon hair was braided in two strands tied by red bows. There was a touch of the Indio in her skin: tan bordering on cocoa. But when she smiled it drew planes on her face that unveiled the Spanish invaders, particularly some Hidalgo beauty in her ancestry: haughty but yet passionate.

No doubt about it, Mrs. Ross thought, Paulita would be devastating the village males right now had not the paralysis taken away most of the use of her legs when she was ten.

Paulita heard the balcony doors. She paused in her work, smiled up at Mrs. Ross. "Good morning," she called, using the English Mrs. Ross had taught her.

"*Buenos días,* Paulita."

Mrs. Ross took up her watering can, stepped through the doorway.

It was then she noticed the American. He stood directly under her in the shadow of the balcony, sketch pad in hand, doing a charcoal drawing of Paulita at the window.

His name came to Mrs. Ross's mind: *Hoblitt, Francis Hoblitt.*

She made it a point to learn the names of all *gringos* who came to San Juan, carefully observed them before she permitted them to see her. Not that she *really* expected anyone from the past to recognize her—what with the changed name and her beauty withered away by the years and sun.

Still … there was always the chance: an old customer, one of her girls. And this was such a simple precaution. It would make things insufferable in San Juan should the natives learn of her past.

Mrs. Ross studied Hoblitt: the intensity of the man at his work—slashing strokes of pencil, blots of black on the paper. The artist was a blond, athletic type with corded muscles showing at the shoulders beneath a white shirt. His features, as Mrs. Ross recalled, were stern, full of angular abruptness. He had been in San Juan only a month, but already was tanned a rich shade of golden oak.

Something about the man plucked at Mrs. Ross's memory. The thought darted away before she could label it. She began watering her plants, tried to recall—*What? Something. It definitely had been something.*

Irritation at the young man touched Mrs. Ross. Usually at this hour she carried on a conversation, back and forth across the street, with Paulita. This morning—Hoblitt standing there—it was out of the question. Paulita was too busy with the eye-dodging game, a type of flirting in which all Mexican young women became adepts starting at the age of three.

From her second-floor vantage, Mrs. Ross could see through Paulita's window to the floor of the Romera house: the crutches beside the chair, the red and black serape thrown across the young woman's almost useless legs. Mrs. Ross knew that the window ledge would conceal these things from the artist. It crossed her mind that this made a more kindly portrayal. Hoblitt saw just a beautiful young woman at her window—very Spanish.

The watering can gurgled its empty signal as Mrs. Ross finished with the last of the chives. She put down the can, leaned over the rail to peer at Hoblitt.

"I see you're an artist," she said, as though she had not known this fact since his second day in the village.

Hoblitt did not answer. He made a slashing mark at the bottom of the sketch, thrust the pad beneath his left arm, stalked off up the street and around the corner. Not once did he look up to see who had spoken.

Mrs. Ross shrugged, smiled at Paulita, took up the brass can, went indoors. She had grown to ignore the ways of her countrymen, especially of the artist-folk who had been appearing lately here in San Juan, at Ajijic, and at Solas. Still—the man's gesture of irritation added to the nagging sureness that there was something about him … something she should remember.

"*Turistas!*" she muttered.

She put the watering can on a chair for Serena to collect, drew the draperies in preparation for the heat of the day. The cloth dulled the sounds from outside.

Now came a special moment in the morning ritual. Through the red-washed gloom, she crossed to a carved Jocotapec sideboard that stood polished and civilized against a plaster wall. There, she mixed herself a glass of Cuban rum and vanilla.

The drink reminded her of the blonde girl who had introduced her to it: Gertie something, an unsmiling Nordic female who hadn't attracted much business. Too intense.

Mrs. Ross sipped her drink.

But that was in another country, and besides the wench is dead, she thought.

A feeling of relaxed satisfaction crept through Mrs. Ross. She took another sip. This time for relaxation was one of the things she had promised herself the day she paid off the girls, withdrawn her savings, and left for the tropics. This and hot sunlight. She began to giggle with an abrupt thought: *Sunlight inside and sunlight outside!*

In that instant, with the laughter still in her throat, memory struck Mrs. Ross. She put down her drink, all pleasure gone from it.

Gertie, of course, she thought. *And seeing that Hoblitt at his work—the way he acts. He's precisely like the young artist who knifed Gertie ... when he found out how she made her living. Even looks like him. Same scowling kind of a face.*

She recalled what the young artist had screamed as the mob dragged him into the night to hang him: *"But she was deformed! She was deformed! I only cut away some filth! Painted filth! Deformed!"*

Mrs. Ross shook her head to drive out the memory of his voice. *The damned fool. Melodramatic to the end ... and so ... empty.*

She looked at her rum and vanilla. *No use going back to it.*

The ritual had been shattered.

Later, she barked at Serena, found fault with the meat at lunch, even snarled at the pair of nuns, mouse-eyed in sexless brown, who came nibbling at her afternoon to collect for church bells.

Word circulated through San Juan: It was one of Mrs. Ross's "days."

The next morning, Hoblitt returned to his position beneath the balcony with a partly completed oil painting and portable easel. There was a stubble of golden beard on his cheeks, paint stained his hands, and he was squinting against the brilliance of the early sunlight as though he had arisen without enough sleep. He wedged the canvas onto the easel, bent to work.

Above him Mrs. Ross fumed. She banged her water can, almost wished she dared spill some on the artist. A restless night had left her in no mood to forgive the arouser of old memories.

Hoblitt wore a white shirt open at the neck, white trousers and tennis sneakers. A blond duck-curl of hair at the nape of his neck lifted when he bent his head. He worked with a smooth sureness that surprised Mrs. Ross. The brush dipped and twisted on the pallet, poised over the canvas—then slid through a controlled flurry of color and shape.

Mrs. Ross glanced across the street, admitted to herself: *He's right—morning light is best.*

It gave Paulita's face a translucent look, put gold flecks in her brown eyes. It bronzed the rust spots on the bars of the iron shutters that stood open against the sides of the window alcove. The red bricks framing the window appeared more red in the early sun, as did the bows in Paulita's hair. And the old plaster of the wall around the window gained a deeper texture from cross lighting.

Paulita was back at the eye-dodging game with the artist this morning. She had interrupted it only long enough to exchange greetings with Mrs. Ross. The girl turned her head as though to look directly at Hoblitt. (She did this almost every time he paused to study the scene.) Then she shifted her attention past him, through him, above him. Never once did she get caught looking directly at him. But she saw him—knew every move he made.

Mrs. Ross finished the watering, put down the brass can with unnecessary noise, peered over the rail. The face on the canvas, seen from this oblique angle, looked to be a clear likeness—not at all the gaudy, sunburst splashes that rioted through Hoblitt's other work on sale at the Tienda Moderna.

The Paulita of the painting sat at her *punto de cruz,* apparently more subdued than in real life, but nonetheless vital and dramatic. She appeared just about to turn her head and look straight out of the picture.

He's caught the eye-dodging game! thought Mrs. Ross.

A sense of grudging admiration filled her. The painting displayed a depth of feeling … and more. With a sense of shock, she realized that this newcomer, this *turista,* had also seen right through to the basic moodiness these people never quite shook off.

Mrs. Ross lifted her head, studied the real girl in the window. The painting had pulled a veil from the scene. She saw the touch of malice lurking in the fawn eyes, the anger lines at the edges of the passionate mouth, the cruelty in the straight Castilian nose. It made Mrs. Ross think of Old Spain and the *señoritas*—the lovely virgins— sitting at their windows: waiting, waiting.

Hoblitt put pallet and brushes onto a rack attached to the cross arm of the easel, turned, stared up at Mrs. Ross. His brows stood out whitely against the tan.

"Don't you have anything else to do besides look over my shoulder?" he asked.

Speechless, Mrs. Ross stiffened with anger.

"Why don't you go stir your kettle or something?" asked Hoblitt. "It's very distracting to have someone looking down like that all the time."

"Well!" exploded Mrs. Ross. She whirled, fled into her house, slammed the French doors. *What an insufferable young man!* Things she should have said tumbled through her mind. *The very idea!* Her anger demanded action. She stalked through the house to the back garden, a space enclosed by high adobe walls and filled with a jungle of green leaves, blue, yellow, and flaming blooms. She grabbed a trowel off the potting table. *Why ... the very idea!* She beat a frenzied rhythm with the trowel on the table. *What gall!* She fought back her fury, turned to the garden, began weeding around the hibiscus.

Shortly before noon, Serena returned from the market. She had been talking to María Carlotta, the Friesmans' maid, who also cleaned for their tenant, Hoblitt.

Serena was short statured, her tubular body encased in a heavy cotton dress of Carmelite brown that reached below the calf. She had big features, high cheekbones. The large nose, without indentation at the bridge, sloped into a flat forehead and oily black hair. This hair was parted in the middle, swept back in two braids that fell almost to her waist. A profile view of Serena looked like one of the carved stone Aztec figures in the Museo Nacional. She spoke a coarse Spanish full of village-isms. And some ancestor had given her a mobile voice that unconsciously imitated whomever she quoted.

"Such a terrible morning in the market," she said. "Pareno again has raised the price of oranges! He has no right! He is an evil man. I have seen him spit during a rainstorm! He will come to no good end."

She moved about the whitewashed kitchen in a determined, mechanical way—unloading her market basket, hanging her shawl on a peg beside the gas stove.

Mrs. Ross, stinking of a patent sunburn lotion (she had worked too long in the garden) watched from the dining room doorway.

The kitchen was a high room (a story and a half) skylighted to the southeast. Serena's sandals echoed *slap-slap-slap* in the space. A pot of beans on a back burner emitted sporadic burps. Aromas of chili, coffee, frying tortillas, onions, and beans overrode the bottled gas smell. There was a residue of odors in the room from all the past meals that seemed to enfold every new aroma.

"The water reservoir is very low today," said Serena. She began stirring something in a bowl. "There was another failure of the generation during the night." (By generation she meant *electrical* generation, a chancy service in San Juan.) "Without the generation the pump of the water could not serve."

Familiar aromas and the glaring, chalky feeling of the kitchen combined with Serena's chatter to lull Mrs. Ross into a semi-trance. She rocked back and forth on her feet as she listened.

"This Señor Hoblitt," said Serena, "María Carlotta says that sometimes he tears up a painting before it is finished." She introduced chopped onion into a reddish-brown sauce simmering on the front of the stove, returned to the *metate* where she began reducing two tomatoes to pulp.

Mrs. Ross murmured automatically: "How brutal." She stirred herself to wakefulness, wondered what would be the fate of Paulita's portrait.

"Yes!" said Serena. "And, you know, María Carlotta saw him rip pages from a perfectly good magazine once … and burn them! And he cursed the pages while they burned!" She cast a baleful glance at Mrs. Ross. "It makes great danger to curse in front of an open fire."

"Truly, a man of no sensitivity," said Mrs. Ross.

"Yes! And when the flowers in his vases wilt, he rages. Such language, God preserve us." Serena crossed herself with a hand dripping redly of tomato. "And then he must have fresh flowers in his room or the walls tremble from his roaring." She shook her head, braids swinging. "A real artist, that one."

Mrs. Ross nodded. Her mind had veered off to the other artist, the one who had killed Gertie. A fearful association began to form in her mind: *This Hoblitt is probably just as empty-headed crazy as the other one. What happens when he discovers that Paulita is … deformed … that her beauty doesn't extend beneath the windowsill?*

She shook her head to clear it. These were insane thoughts. But she wondered then if it might not be best to visit Don Jaime, have the source of the irritation removed—perhaps deported.

Serena began loading a tray with food, said: "Someone should warn that man: it makes the most terrible danger to remove dead flowers from a house except after dark." She lifted the tray. *"Comida!"*

Mrs. Ross stepped aside for Serena to pass. *I'll visit Paulita this afternoon*, she thought. *Perhaps she could complain to Don Jaime.*

Chapter 3

In the courtyard of Paulita Romera's home a somnolent humming of insects arose from potted flowers around the arcade edge. It was an old house (more than two hundred years) built of adobe and hand-carved beams. A curious interlacing of odors filled the place: mouldy earth, a sharp touch of charcoal smoke, faint acridity from the pigsty and chicken pens out back behind an organ cactus fence—all dominated by the hothouse aromas of flowers.

The old aunt who cared for Paulita, a bent and withered creature in a brown dress of the same cut as Serena's, admitted Mrs. Ross with a murmured, *"Buenas tardes."* Mrs. Ross could hear the *pat-pat-pat* of someone making tortillas. There was the dry whisking of a broom coming from one of the rooms opening onto the arcade. The aunt clanged the *caonzel* gate behind them, motioned to where Paulita, wearing a red blouse and with a faded green robe over her legs, sat sewing in the shaded area outside the *sala*.

An arch of Moorish fretwork framed the girl's position. The *punto de cruz* was a red and yellow splash on her lap. Her crutches leaned against a nearby column from which paint was peeling in scabrous patches.

"Good afternoon," called Paulita. She spoke English because she felt it gratified Mrs. Ross to see how her only student had retained the lessons.

"Good afternoon, Paulita." Mrs. Ross acquiesced to the choice of tongues, but secretly bridled at the constrictions in English. The thoughts she wanted to convey could be said with more delicate fulsomeness in Spanish.

"It is such a hot day," said Paulita. "Come into the shade."

Mrs. Ross crossed the courtyard, thought about the insight to Paulita's character revealed by the portrait: the cruelty, the iron pride, the malice. A sense of outrage at the artist came over her, as though she had caught a peeping Tom at the window.

The aunt scurried up with a cane chair from the *sala*, effaced herself with a murmurous, "Dispense me." She retired to the back of the house, long skirt swishing about her black-clad ankles.

"Do sit down," said Paulita.

Mrs. Ross resigned herself to the creaking, angular chair, felt it bite into the backs of her legs. *Mexican furniture!* she thought, sighing.

"It has been hot," she said. "I'll be glad when the rains start."

"The lake is very low this year," said Paulita. She bit off a thread, glanced sidelong at Mrs. Ross. "You've come to talk about the artist. I saw you watching him this morning."

The girl displayed a decidedly un-Spanish directness when she spoke English, Mrs. Ross thought. She wondered if there might not be an inherent straightness to the language, said: "He strikes me as a very boorish person."

"I heard what he said to you," said Paulita. "But I'm sure he means no harm. It is merely ..." she shrugged. "... that he is so concerned about his work. Artists, you know." She glanced down, plucked at a tuft in the robe over her legs.

"Perhaps he doesn't mean any harm," said Mrs. Ross. "But I still think he's boorish. Did he ask you if he could paint your portrait?"

"No. We have not spoken." Paulita looked up, bent towards Mrs. Ross, dark eyes glistening. "But you have seen the portrait! Is it a good likeness?"

How like a Latin woman! thought Mrs. Ross. "Quite a passable likeness," she admitted.

"I knew it!" Paulita sat back. "He takes so much time with everything—mixing the paints, testing. She giggled.

"Did you see how he dripped paint all over his hands?"

"Don't you think it's rude to paint your picture without asking permission?" countered Mrs. Ross.

It was as though Paulita had not heard. "And is he not a handsome young man?" she asked. "So fierce in the eyes!"

"To be sure," murmured Mrs. Ross. A mosquito whined above her left wrist. She slapped it, recoiled at the stinging in her sunburn. *That damnable young man!* It was obvious that Paulita would never complain. Mrs. Ross realized that she would have to take the matter up with Don Jaime herself.

But what can I tell him? she wondered.

Paulita drew in a deep breath that filled her red blouse with nubile bust line. "I wish I could see the painting," she sighed.

A pang touched Mrs. Ross. The girl had so few pleasures, and this painting obviously intrigued her. She still talked of the photographer who had taken her portrait in color for the magazine Revista Nacional.

But the photographer, being Mexican, had asked permission. Mrs. Ross hardened her heart. *There's inherent tragedy in this situation,* she told herself. *This poor girl is being led to dream foolish things. And here she is … deformed, and without …*

Abruptly, Mrs. Ross saw how to present the problem to Don Jaime.

I will see him tomorrow! she thought.

CHAPTER 4

In his parlor, Don Jaime turned away from the copper puddle of sun reflection the lake, brushed the fly from his hair, cleared his throat.

Mrs. Ross stirred out of her reverie, glanced at her jeweled lapel watch. Less than a minute had passed.

"Emma, my dearest friend," said Don Jaime in his lisping Spanish, "it is that you fear the young man will do harm to Paulita, no?"

"Precisely."

"But you cannot be certain of this thing."

"Who would take a chance in such a matter?" demanded Mrs. Ross.

Don Jaime pursed his lips, pinched in his cheeks. He looked more than ever like the figure of the crucifix.

"But, of course. However, I would very much like to see this painting."

Mrs. Ross stiffened. She had learned to be wary of Don Jaime's digressions when coming to a point.

"A natural desire, no?" asked Don Jaime.

"What do you propose?" asked Mrs. Ross.

"I will use all of the tact of which I am capable," said Don Jaime. "I will be the soul and heart of discretion. We will be together, the artist and I, with the painting before us. What could be more natural than to lead the conversation around to Paulita's tragic condition?"

"God preserve us!" blurted Mrs. Ross. "That's the very thing you mustn't do!"

"But why not?"

"I told you what the other artist did when he learned of the girl's deformity!" (Mrs. Ross had altered the story of Gertie slightly, then realized that possibly the girl *had* been deformed—although not in a physical sense.)

Don Jaime's brows contracted in a puzzled frown. He thought: *It is possible that the young man does not know about Paulita's legs. But could it make such a difference as that?*

"It this a characteristic of all artists from América del Norte?" he asked.

"Only of a certain type," said Mrs. Ross. "And this one shows all the symptoms of being that type."

Don Jaime nodded. "To be sure." And then so low that Mrs. Ross almost missed it: *"Gringos!"*

"You have come to a decision?" ventured Mrs. Ross.

A sigh convulsed Don Jaime's thin chest. "As God wills it." He raised a finger. "But such things take time! It must be done with circumspection." Then, to let Mrs. Ross know that he was not an utter fool: "… not like the one who had to go to the hospital."

Mrs. Ross coughed, raised a hand to her mouth to hide a smile. She composed herself, lowered the hand. "I knew I could trust you, Jaime. You have so much experience in matters of the world, such a penetrating mind. You're the only one who can handle this in a way that will avert tragedy."

"You are too kind," murmured Don Jaime. And he thought: *Could it be? Is this possible? The young man appears so talented—so simpático.*

CHAPTER 5

The next morning, Friday, Mrs. Ross again found Hoblitt bent over his easel in the shade of the balcony when she emerged to water her plants.

The brush moved at a furious rate: dip and stroke, dip and stroke. Little rivers of color blended into the portrait. Paulita's figure appeared almost completed, but the background still showed raw patches of canvas.

Fortified by her angry reveries, Mrs. Ross thought: *Just say something to me today, Mr. Smart Alec! I'll burn your ears off!*

But Hoblitt ignored her presence.

Mrs. Ross sniffed. *Paint away, fool! You'll be gone soon.*

Paulita executed and advanced ploys in the eye-dodging game, looked up at the balcony. "Good morning, Mrs. Ross."

"*Buenos días*, Paulita."

It stopped there, inhibited by the presence beneath the balcony.

Mrs. Ross smiled, though, paused to admire Paulita. The young woman still worked at the *punto de cruz*. A great red poinsettia was emerging beneath her needle. She wore green bows in her hair this morning, but Mrs. Ross noted that Hoblitt thus far had ignored the color change. The bows of the painting remained red.

The easel creaked as Hoblitt adjusted its position, studied the scene.

Paulita stopped to thread a needle, used the diversion for a series of new gambits in eye-dodging.

Mrs. Ross shook her head in admiration. She could not be certain because of the angle, but she thought she saw Hoblitt grin before he again bent to his work. For no reason she could explain, this sent Mrs. Ross's thoughts into the penetrating character analysis emerging beneath the artist's brush: passionate but cruel—that was the Paulita of the portrait.

Anger flared in Mrs. Ross. *A damnable young man! Coming in here without asking! Disrupting a nice, orderly life!*

She slammed the French doors as she went inside.

Chapter 6

At noon, Serena bustled in, her shopping basket on one thick, brown arm. The basket bulged with toma-toes, bananas, a brown paper package of meat, a stack of tortillas wrapped in cloth, onions, oranges, a mound of green chili peppers. She began recounting her morning's net of gossip as she unloaded the basket onto the grey boards of the kitchen table.

"In the evening of yesterday," she said, "Don Jaime made for himself a visit to the Señor Hoblitt."

Mrs. Ross experienced a cold sensation in her stomach. She stood in the doorway to the dining room, just out of the chalk glare that always filled the kitchen at mid-day.

"And María Carlotta, who delivered some fruit to the little house just then, saw them drinking together—gin and limes in the large glasses!"

Mrs. Ross's lips formed the automatic reply: "How brutal."

"And they looked at a painting which the Señor Hoblitt keeps in a locked box when he is not working on it. Don Jaime said he likes this painting very much."

"You mean the portrait of Paulita," sad Mrs. Ross.

"No, Señora." Serena crossed to the sink, began rinsing tomatoes in a bowl of water. She spoke over her shoulder: "This is another one. This is probably the one Don Jaime is buying."

"Buying?" Mrs. Ross stared at Serena's brown-clad back, the two dark braids jerking like animated bell-pulls.

"Yes. María Carlotta says that Don Jaime buys one of the paintings, but she has not seen it. The *Señor* Hoblitt keeps it in the locked box."

The mystery of this caught Mrs. Ross's interest. And, for some reason, it disquieted her. She thought: *What did that fool Jaime say to Hoblitt?*

She said: "Did not María Carlotta overhear their conversation?"

"Not very much of it, Señora." Serena crossed to the stove with an earthen bowl which she sat on a rear burner. "The Señor Hoblitt ordered María Carlotta from the house, although he had not completed sorting his fruit. She heard them laughing, however, as she left." Serena lowered her voice, peered at Mrs. Ross from slitted eyes. "They were discussing espionage! María Carlotta heard the word, and that is all she cares to say about it."

Espionage? Mrs. Ross shook her head sharply. She felt that the sense of the conversation had veered off into a region where she could not follow.

"Espionage!" repeated Serena. She returned to the sink for another bowl.

Mrs. Ross felt an unexplainable tightness in her throat, wondered if she was coming down with one of the recurrent tropic maladies that she wrote off as the price of the sunshine.

Serena shuffled back to the stove, poured meat stock into the earthen pot, turned up the gas flame, faced Mrs. Ross. The Aztec features looked flat and avid. "The Señor Hoblitt has given to María Carlotta two positively new pairs of nylons," she said. She looked accusingly at her employer, who only released nylons when they had runs and must be repaired by the girl in the Tienda Moderna at a cost of fifty centavos each.

Mrs. Ross pulled at her lower lip. She was thinking about Don Jaime's visit to Hoblitt. *Two hours together! And not the first time, evidently.* Then: *Espionage?*

Serena's last announcement registered slowly, expanding like a balloon until it burst on Mrs. Ross's consciousness: Two pairs of new nylons! A bribe!

Espionage! It occurred to Mrs. Ross that the kitchen-maid grapevine in San Juan worked in two directions.

"Has the Señor Hoblitt been asking questions about me?" she demanded.

Serena's expression drifted into bland vacuity. "I cannot say, Señora. Maybe yes, maybe no."

Even if she did know she wouldn't tell me! thought Mrs. Ross. She realized that she had violated a basic rule of the grapevine: one did not suggest even remotely that one's own servant revealed private confidences.

Serena turned away, fussed with the stove.

Mrs. Ross stared at the woman's implacable back. At least once a day Serena extinguished the gas flame by trying to coax more heat out of it by fanning it like a charcoal fire. *The stupid!*

"I'm not feeling well," said Mrs. Ross. "I'll just have some soup. You may serve me in the bedroom."

She left before Serena could begin detailing all the deaths from various incurable blights that had stricken San Juan the previous month.

And it wouldn't do a bit of good to question Don Jaime, Mrs. Ross thought as she climbed the stairs to her bedroom. *He's close up just like Serena. When you get right down to it, they're all alike! Always gossiping! No one's safe from it!*

The bedroom looked shadowy and inviting with all the blinds pulled. Thin strips of slatted light wavered across the bedspread, climbed up the tall mahogany *ropero* where she kept her clothes on *gringo* hangers. The bedspread was one Paulita had made: blue herons cross-stitched on a white background.

Mrs. Ross sat on the edge of the bed, rubbed a hand across the rough surface beside her. The sore throat was growing more pronounced. She sensed the hush outside that came over San Juan at siesta time. A sigh lifted her shoulders.

Perhaps I've been pushing myself too hard lately, she thought. Maybe I should spend a few days in bed. It doesn't pay to take chances with these Mexican germs.

She lay back on the bed, her thought growing to decision. *Just a day or two in bed.* She yawned, listening for Serena with the luncheon tray. And the thought occurred to her that she would be besieged by little cups and bowls of herbal remedies if she stayed in bed. Two tribulations of being ill in San Juan were the sudden martinet officiousness of Serena and the procession of native medicines delivered by narrow-faced girl children with dirty legs and wearing oversized hand-me-down head shawls.

And there was no stopping Serena's outpouring of epidemic calamities, each closed by the ominous portents that had warned of disaster: "… if only they had known."

CHAPTER 7

On Sunday, the second morning of Mrs. Ross's "illness," Serena entered the sick chamber at eight-thirty, shouldering the door open while she protected the breakfast tray in her thick arms. She wore an orange bib apron over her black "church" dress. Her braids were tied off by two bits of silver ribbon rescued from a Christmas wrapping the previous year. On the tray was the diet she considered fitting for the ill: two eggs coddled in milk, orange juice, one piece of dry toast. And instead of coffee, she had brought this morning a cup of Jamaica tea looking faintly pinkish in a yellow cup.

Mrs. Ross had been awake since the first church bells had begun calling to Mass at five-thirty. But there was no way to get Serena to bring breakfast earlier.

"The sick need more sleep!" Serena would say. Then would come the calamitous case histories of those who had ignored this warning.

Mrs. Ross listened to Serena's sandals slapping across the tile floor, heard them go mute on the serape-rug. She turned, looked up at the maid.

Serena's Aztec face held a look of pleased grief. There was a small bandage on the middle finger of her right hand. She had burned herself at the gas stove the previous day. Mrs. Ross knew that the bandage would stay there at least two days past the point of complete healing—a reminder of martyrdom.

"Father Aguilar said Mass for the repose of Hector Reliquero's soul this morning," said Serena.

Mrs. Ross blinked. "Oh?" Then she remembered: *Reliquero—that's the young fisherman from Solas who drowned.*

Serena put the breakfast tray on the nightstand while she raised the blinds at the window beside the bed half way. (To raise window blinds all the way in a sick room created great danger.) Still, there was a warm wash of sunshine across the edge of the bed. Mrs. Ross bathed a hand in it. Serena bent, helped her employer sit up, adjusted the nightgown worn at these times as a concession to propriety.

The glow of sunlight failed to dispel a cold gloom that dripped from the maid's every motion as she deposited the tray in Mrs. Ross's lap.

"On the radio, it was said that an entire busload of religious pilgrims was killed in an accident near Oaxaca last night," she announced.

Mrs. Ross grimaced. Yesterday, it had been the collapse of a building in Italy. Serena's recording-device memory switched automatically to these things at the first hint of sickness. Global news services kept her saturated with avalanches, floods, train accidents, hotel fires....

"Anyone from San Juan on the bus?" asked Mrs. Ross.

"They have not yet released the names of the dead." Serena folded her arms, stared at the breakfast tray.

Alerted, Mrs. Ross studied the array of food, noted the washed-out pinkish-brown of what should have been a cup of coffee. She pointed to it. "What's that?"

"Jamaica tea, Señora."

"Jamaica tea?"

"My sainted mother, Señora, if only we had given her Jamaica tea soon enough, I am sure she would not have died when she did." Serena crossed herself.

"Take it away."

"But Señora!" Serena stiffened into her martinet pose. "It has a delicious flavor and ..."

"I said take it away!"

Even martinets wilted at this tone. Serena sniffed, as much as to say: *Let your death be on your own shoulders then!* She put the offending cup on the nightstand.

"Well, what are you waiting for?" demanded Mrs. Ross.

Serena's face retained an impassive scowl. She dipped a hand into the pocket of her orange apron, produced a thin package wrapped in tan kraft paper. "The Señor Hoblitt sends you this." She held it out. "It is a picture."

Mrs. Ross accepted the offering. Hoblitt? She unfolded the paper. It crackled, and one corner tore. Inside there lay a tempera crayon sketch of herself. The features were drawn boldly without background, but the artist had removed about twenty years from her age: more pink in the complexion, fewer wrinkles around the eyes, cheeks fuller, hair a dark auburn-red.

The portrayal looked very much like the Emma Ross who had come to San Juan in nineteen-thirty-seven. For several heartbeats, Mrs. Ross wondered if this might be Hoblitt's subtle way of telling her that he knew all. Then she calmed herself, thinking: The man isn't capable of such subtlety. Still, she wondered: Who told him what color my hair used to be? That's something he couldn't get just from looking at me.

"A good likeness, no?" said Serena. "It looks just the way you did when you first came to us." She nodded. "If you do not want the little portrait, Señora, perhaps you could give it to me. It would be very nice to have." (And the tone of Serena's voice added: "… after you are dead.")

Mrs. Ross shook her head, studied the sketch. She saw the same kind of character penetration that was revealed in the painting of Paulita and was repelled by it. There was a heavy-lidded, furtive look to her eyes, a sense of watchfulness in the set of the head.

"Was there a message?" asked Mrs. Ross.

Serena spoke stiffly, angered by the casual denial of her request: "It is on the back."

Mrs. Ross turned the sketch over, saw there in a scrawling hand: "I apologize for snapping at you. Blame it on a lousy breakfast that day. Let's be friends."

How very odd, thought Mrs. Ross. She turned back to the drawing. It was an irritating thing, not at all the way she pictured herself. A thought struck her. She said: "Has this Hoblitt made a large painting of me, Serena?"

"Who knows?" Serena shrugged. "María Carlotta says there are other paintings which the Señor Hoblitt keeps in a locked box. It is said that he prepares them for the show by foreign artists to be held soon at the University of Mexico. It is next week, I think."

Mrs. Ross lifted her attention from the sketch, stared at the *ropero* opposite the foot of the bed, thought: *If he's made a large portrait like that and displays it at a public showing …* She shuddered. *God knows who might see it!*

Serena cleared her throat.

I must do something, thought Mrs. Ross. *If he has made such a portrait, perhaps I could buy …*

Again, Serena cleared her throat.

"What is it?" demanded Mrs. Ross.

"Don Jaime has sent Dr. Herrera to examine you."

Anger flared in Mrs. Ross. "That miserable incompetent! Why does Don Jaime always have to send him? Tell the fool to go back where he came from!"

Secure in the knowledge of past victories, Serena raised her attention to the ceiling. "He awaits even now outside your door, Señora." She sighed. "Within the sound of your voice."

"Let him wait! And bring me some coffee!" Mrs. Ross took up her toast, dipped it into the milk and coddled egg, began eating. She thought: *I wonder how much money Hoblitt would want for ...*

"But coffee makes danger before a visit of the doctor!" Serena looked horrified that Mrs. Ross would not remember this witch signal of disaster.

Mrs. Ross swallowed a bite of her food, took a deep breath, composed herself. She recalled a similar argument during her previous illness. But she had learned even before that how to meet such situations. One did not lunge into them head on: one rolled with the punch.

"If I must see the doctor to get my coffee, then I must," said Mrs. Ross. "Send the fool in, then bring me the coffee."

"If the doctor says it is permitted," countered Serena.

Mrs. Ross closed her eyes, held her temper. The effort showed in the tightness of her voice: "I will see Dr. Herrera."

"Yes, Señora." Serena bowed herself out of the room backward, as though withdrawing from the presence of royalty.

Dr. Herrera replaced her in the doorway, strode into the room, calling out: "Ah, ha, what have we here?" His Spanish was full of dropped endings, short vowels—the Mexico City accent.

"Indisposition, no more," snapped Mrs. Ross. She took a final bite of the toast, put the tray beside her on the bed.

The doctor put his bag on the floor, pulled up a cane chair. It creaked under him. Dr. Herrera was a large man—both tall and broad—with a square, heavy-jowled face, Indian-black hair touched by grey at the temple. He radiated a confidence that soothed sick tourists. Beyond a few medical terms, the doctor spoke perhaps fifteen words of English. Among them: "Hello there." "Good-bye now." and "Take this as directed."

"No malaise of the stomach?" he asked. (Dr. Herrera was convinced, with some justification, that most North Americans' medical problems originated in the stomach or intestines.)

"I'm not a tourist!" barked Mrs. Ross.

"But, of course," said Dr. Herrera. "Was I not in the courtroom on the day you became a citizen of our beloved country?"

"Maybe you were," agreed Mrs. Ross. Then: "You'll notice they didn't expropriate *my* properties!"

"To be sure." Dr. Herrera put a hand to her forehead, looked thoughtful. "The appetite is good?"

"Yes! If that fool Serena would only fix me some decent food."

The doctor took his hand away, patted the edge of the bed. "The indisposition: does it pain you in any particular place?"

Mrs. Ross felt that she was being bullied. She pushed back into the pillows, muttered almost against her will: "A little soreness of the throat, no more."

"Ah, but one must not leave these things unattended." One of Dr. Herrera's ape-like arms reached down to the floor beside him. He unsnapped the bag, removed a tongue-depressor. "Let us observe the throat, eh?"

"It's not that bad," protested Mrs. Ross. And, indeed, she could barely feel the soreness that had kept her wakefully irritated during the night.

"All the same," insisted Dr. Herrera. He moved the depressor toward her mouth.

Mrs. Ross found herself going through the ridiculous routine of saying, "Ahhhhh." It made her cough.

When the coughing spell subsided, Dr. Herrera said: "I will send the girl with an injection. You have picked up a little virus. There is some around here just now."

"No injections!" protested Mrs. Ross.

Dr. Herrera ignored the interruption. He removed a glass tube of pills from his bag. "And here is some *Viotalidina,* just in case there is an involvement of the stomach, eh? I will leave these with Serena. One little *pastilla* every four hours. And you must increase your intake of liquids."

"Let Serena take the pills," growled Mrs. Ross. Then: "Oh, and tell her it's permitted for me to have coffee."

Dr. Herrera grasped the bag, lifted his bulk out of the cane chair. He smiled, a tourist-soothing, confident expression that made him look like a Buddha with hair. "But of course. You will drink the coffee to wash down the *pastillas.*" He bowed. "I will look in on you in two days."

Mrs. Ross, seeing that she would pay for her coffee by swallowing the pills, started to protest, then resigned herself to the inevitable. It occurred to her that the Mexicans *always* rolled with a punch. *Trained to it from infancy!* she thought.

"Goodbye now," recited Dr. Herrera in English.

Serena returned after showing the doctor to the door. She brought coffee and one of the pills. A look of gleeful malice filled her face—especially around the eyes. "The doctor says …"

"I know what the doctor says!"

Mrs. Ross gulped the pill, shuddered, sipped her coffee. Presently, she said: "Is that Hoblitt still painting out there?"

"The portrait of Señorita Paulita grows more beautiful by the minute," said Serena. "Such an artist, that one!"

Mrs. Ross glanced at the sketch lying face up on her nightstand. *He probably charges outrageous prices for his work,* she thought. *And wouldn't I look the fool going out there to ask if he's painted my picture! Simply outrageous prices. I'd look like a vain old woman. Especially if he hadn't painted my picture. And he most likely hasn't. When could he have painted it? He hasn't been standing around mooning at me the way he has with Paulita.*

She sat there, wrestling with the weak remnants of her previous worry.

Serena said: "Is there anything you wish, Señora?"

"Just a moment, just a moment." Mrs. Ross reached out, reversed the sketch, studied Hoblitt's message.

Peace offering, hmmmph! she thought. *He's just found out how rich I am. Probably thinks I'll come right out with this little sketch and spend a thousand dollars hiring him to paint a big one like it. Well, he can just think again.*

"Our street is very busy for a Sunday," said Serena.

"Oh?" Mrs. Ross relaxed against her pillows, thought: Jaime will get rid of him. I must put more faith in Jaime.

Serena said: "Already this morning there have passed …" She ticked them off on her fingers: "… the Señor Iriarte, the Señora Aguilar y Cantido, the Señor Muñoz with his Señora, the Señoritas Castillano, the entire familia García, the …"

"All gawking at that fool painting," said Mrs. Ross. And she thought: *They're all curious about the picture of Paulita. That's all it is. Jaime was curious, too, nothing more.*

"There is curiosity about the portrait," said Serena.

That's all it was, thought Mrs. Ross. *Jaime was curious. And, fool that he is, he let that insufferable young man sell him a painting. Probably paid ten pesos for it, too.*

Mrs. Ross finished her coffee. "What time did Señor Hoblitt arrive to paint this morning?"

"Shortly after eight, Señora."

"What Mass did the Señorita Paulita attend?"

"But she always attends the first Mass at five-thirty, Señora." Serena appeared puzzled. "I saw her there myself."

"Then Señor Hoblitt did not see Paulita outside … on her crutches."

"Oh!" Serena shook her head, braids dancing. "He is like all artists: a late ariser. María Carlotta says he seldom gets himself up before seven-thirty."

Mrs. Ross nodded.

"Is it wrong that Señor Hoblitt should see the Señorita on her crutches?" asked Serena. She half-turned her head, bent forward. One braid slipped over her shoulder to swing in front of Mrs. Ross—a silver-bowed pendulum.

Mrs. Ross eyed the braid, succumbed to inspiration. "It makes great danger," she muttered.

"Ahhhh!" Serena jerked upright, eyes growing large. "It makes great danger for an artist to see someone on crutches!"

CHAPTER 8

T he very worst kind of danger," said Mrs. Ross. "Now, run and get me some more coffee." She snuggled against the pillows, hugged private enjoyment from the fact that Don Jaime had sent the doctor. He always did. Still … it was a warm gesture.

o o o

The next morning—Monday—Serena appeared with the breakfast tray: coffee in a pale green cup, the pill sitting in its own little yellow bowl like a magenta seed in a blossom. She raised the shades to their sick-room half-mast, helped her employer sit up, swooped the tray onto the waiting lap.

A dollop of coffee sloshed onto the saucer.

Mrs. Ross frowned at the spilled coffee, frowned even deeper at the pill, waited for the morning's seasoning of death and destruction.

"It is a beautiful day," said Serena.

Mrs. Ross looked up, wondered: *What now?* Serena was smiling.

"The eggs are very fresh," said Serena. "The Señora Gonzales had some extra that she permitted me to buy."

She's trying to distract me, thought Mrs. Ross. *She's put something in the food.*

"I will make your favorite tamales for lunch," said Serena.

Mrs. Ross picked up the dishes one at a time, sniffed their contents. Serena took this opportunity to fluff the pillows behind her employer's head.

"What medicine have you introduced into my food?" demanded Mrs. Ross.

"But nothing, Señora! Only the pill which Dr. Herrera says you must take with the coffee."

Mrs. Ross stared the flat Aztec face, cast through her memory of experiences with Serena. There had to be a clue to this unnatural happiness in a sickroom. What was the switch that turned off Calamity Jane? She had it: a dream! That's what had done it the last time.

"You've had a dream," said Mrs. Ross. She took up her fork, snared a bit of egg floating in the milk.

"But no, Señora! Last night I slept the dreamless sleep of a blessed infant."

Mrs. Ross swallowed the bite of egg. "Why are you so happy, then? Have you …"

"Happy?" Serena's features sagged. "Who could be happy on this day? Last night …" Her voice cracked. "… last night an avalanche took the lives of seventy-one helpless innocents in the mountains of Switzerland."

Well … that's more like it, thought Mrs. Ross. She turned back to the breakfast, hesitated, said: "Is that Hoblitt still painting out front?"

Serena brightened. "No, Señora. He works in his rooms. But already today I have seen him.

"Oh?" Mrs. Ross studied the maid's face. It was as though two puppet-masters fought for control of Serena's expression: one pulling up, one pulling down. The happiness mask triumphed. Serena beamed.

Mrs. Ross said: "Where have you seen him?"

"I delivered some of the eggs from Mrs. Gonzales to María Carlotta," said Serena. "You do not mind?"

"Of course not. What happened?"

Serena put a hand to her breast. "The Señor Hoblitt desires to do a portrait of *me!*"

God in heaven! thought Mrs. Ross. She said: "He asked you to pose for him?"

"Yes. With María Carlotta. He desires to portray us at the laundry tubs … together. Is it not an honor?" She half turned her head, looked archly at Mrs. Ross. "Such an artist!"

"And when are you supposed to do this posing?" asked Mrs. Ross.

"It will be only for an hour in the mornings," said Serena. "I will start earlier with my work for you. It will not discomfort you in any way."

Mrs. Ross fumed. She thought: *Now! When Jaime rids us of this beastly young man, I will have to contend with Serena's moping about because her picture was not painted.*

"I will let nothing evil befall you," said Serena.

"Artists have been known to change their minds," said Mrs. Ross. "Don't get your hopes up."

"You will see," said Serena. "You will truly see."

"Yes, we'll see," said Mrs. Ross.

"Well, I must get to my work," said Serena. "There is much to do." She turned away humming. And at the door, she did a little dance step that made her tubular body almost appear light and dainty.

That damnable young man! thought Mrs. Ross.

CHAPTER 9

Shortly after noon, Serena waltzed into the sickroom with the luncheon tray. A slender blue vase containing three yellow roses graced the center of the tray.

"Your tamales, Señora," said Serena as she deposited the tray in Mrs. Ross's lap, whisked a napkin off the plate. "Sweet ones," she announced. "Just the way you like them."

Mrs. Ross put aside the pocketbook she had been reading (a Spanish imitation of the English-language mystery thriller entitled *Parachute to Death!*). She admired the mound of tamales in their cornhusk sheathes. Steam curled upward from them. And at one side there was another mound of beans with cheese, some green peas, and a sweetbread roll. The pill rested on the edge of the saucer beside the coffee cup.

"How very nice the food looks," said Mrs. Ross.

"The Señor Hoblitt goes away," said Serena.

In the act of reaching for her fork, Mrs. Ross stopped, looked up, saw no sadness on Serena's face. For all that it showed in her expression, the woman could just as well have announced an increase in production by Mrs. Gonzales's chickens.

"The artist?" inquired Mrs. Ross. "He is leaving San Juan?"

"Yes. Even now he is packing." Serena maintained her look of bland unconcern.

She is presenting a brave front for my benefit, thought Mrs. Ross. She said: "And what of the painting he was to do of you and María Carlotta?"

Serena shrugged. "As you said: artists are fickle."

"And where does he go?" asked Mrs. Ross.

"Away."

"Yes, but where?"

"Who knows?"

"I see." Mrs. Ross recognized Serena's reply. It was the one frequently used when she knew an answer but refused to reveal it. On occasion, though, it meant no more than it suggested.

"Then you do not know where he is going?" pressed Mrs. Ross.

"He has not told *me,* Señora."

"To be sure." Mrs. Ross recognized the futility of further questioning. "Well …" She straightened against the pillows.

"Careful, Señora!" Serena rescued the vase of roses which was teetering on the tray. She put the vase on the bedside stand.

Mrs. Ross smiled. No matter where Hoblitt went: he was going. By Mexican standards, Jaime had achieved miraculous speed in ridding them of the artist. Mrs. Ross felt rested, her appetite sharp.

"I think I will try getting up for lunch today," she said.

Serena's braids flung themselves about with the violent shaking of her head. "Dr. Herrera said …"

"Dr. Herrera does not run my life! Bring me my robe. Hmmmph. The man barely knows one pill from another."

Later in the afternoon, Mrs. Ross ventured across the cobblestones to visit Paulita. It was a dampish, hot day and the humidity gave a cloying quality to all the tropic aromas, sharpened the bitter odors of decay. She felt a sense of escape as she stepped into the shadows of the Romera doorway.

Paulita sat at her accustomed place beneath the Moorish fretwork that framed the entrance to her *sala.* A white serape draped her legs. All around her—the courtyard lush with flowers and a riot of greenery, the somnolence of humming insects and muted house sounds—there was an air of relaxation. But Paulita's fingers, darting the needle across the red splash of poinsettia, betrayed a secret frenzy, out of tune with her surroundings. And the Hidalgo ancestress stood out prominently in her today: the flaring nostrils, quick movements of the head, the proud way she straightened in the chair to greet her visitor.

"But you are better!" she called in English while Mrs. Ross was crossing the courtyard. "We were so worried about you."

Mrs. Ross resigned herself to the sharp-edged cane chair facing Paulita, took a deep breath. The afternoons were so muggy this time of year. She noted the perspireation dotting Paulita's forehead, the bubbling-over in the girl's manner.

"I'm feeling much better, thank you," said Mrs. Ross. And she wondered: *What is wrong with the girl?*

"We sent Carmella with a cup of herb soup," said Paulita.

Mrs. Ross recalled ordering Serena out of the room with the offering. "It was delicious," she said. She fanned herself. In spite of the uncomfortable chair, it felt good to be sitting.

"It will rain soon," said Paulita. "It is so damp." She returned to her needlework, cast sidelong glances at Mrs. Ross.

She acts exactly like someone with a secret, thought Mrs. Ross.

Paulita bit off a thread, peered toward the back of the house, returned her attention to Mrs. Ross. "I have a note from him," she hissed.

"A note? From …" The implications exploded in Mrs. Ross's consciousness.

Paulita hunched her shoulders in a giggle that made her look school-girlish. "Yes. He sent it by Antonio Muñoz. Antonio was not supposed to tell anyone except me who sent him, but my aunt is his godmother. She made him tell her."

Mrs. Ross swallowed with difficulty. "What did …"

"He paid Antonio five pesos to bring the note!"

"I see. And what did he say in the note?" Mrs. Ross felt her sore throat returning.

"He said he had to go away for a while, but that he would return and bring me something to make me happy! Is it not exciting?" She lapsed into Spanish, speaking at a furious rate: "What a brute in the eyes! Auntie was outraged. We have not been introduced. We know nothing about him. Remember that artist who … you know … with Ferencia Alabano." Paulita hugged her *punto de cruz* to her nubile bosom. "Oh, how exciting it is!"

What has gone wrong? wondered Mrs. Ross. *Something is definitely wrong.* She recalled Serena's unnatural reaction to the artist's departure, said: "Paulita, my dear, I know this type of young man. Artists are a strange …"

"Oh, you're just like Auntie!" exploded Paulita. "She thinks …" She glanced at the spindly outline of her legs beneath the serape. "… just because I must use the sticks to walk that I cannot have … a real life."

"Perhaps all this is possible," ventured Mrs. Ross. "But what happens when the young man discovers …" She, too, glanced at the serape.

Paulita smiled. A knowing expression came over her proud face. "It is not just the legs that a young man admires. Surely you know this?"

But Mrs. Ross's thoughts were twisting through their own private horror. She had convinced herself that Hoblitt, when he learned of Paulita's infirmity, would react as the other young artist had reacted: *Beauty with a deformity must be destroyed! Let no deformity survive!* She envisioned Hoblitt: jaws slavering, knife upraised, advancing on a cowering Paulita. It was a scene modified by the Gertie experience but otherwise lifted out of a B movie starring Lon Chaney that she had seen twenty-five years before.

"It must not be!" she muttered.

Paulita bent to her sewing. "What will be, will be," she said. There was a mixture of Indian fatalism and the Hidalgo beauty poring over her secrets in Paulita's manner. "God has many plans," she said.

In great agitation, Mrs. Ross arose, said: "I must be going. I just remembered that I have to see Don Jaime."

"Oh …" Paulita straightened. "But you have just arrived."

"Please forgive me, child," said Mrs. Ross. "But it is something that I forgot."

"Well, if you must," said Paulita.

The journey across the village went with maddening slowness. In the first place, there was the hot, muggy afternoon. Secondly, the three days in bed had sapped her strength. Each succeeding curb seemed higher than the one before, and the cobblestones were like live things that lay in wait to make her stumble. But even worse than these was the way every doorway, with its waiting villager, drained away the minutes.

"But you are recovered!"

It was the fat, oily-skinned Señora Puntarilla, wife of the village pharmacist. She blocked the narrow sidewalk like a wall, slab arms outstretched in joy.

Mrs. Ross stopped, hid exasperation behind a smile. There was no way around the woman short of detouring through the cobblestone street with its litter of burro droppings. One simply did not do that.

"I offered a candle and my prayers," said Señora Puntarilla. "And God has answered!"

It took easily two minutes to get the woman to turn sideways, opening a way past.

By that time the alert was out, and each doorway held its waiting greeter: "What a miracle!" "We prayed for you!" "The Jamaica tea: that is what did it. When my aunt …"

She came at last to the two-story cream stucco and glass brick monolith that Don Jaime used both as residence and city hall. Behind a tall iron fence and a garden massed with cabbage palms, hibiscus, bougain-villea, agave and countless vines and creepers, the house reared up like some robot monster lifting itself to peer out at the lake. The second floor windows looked glassy and staring.

Mrs. Ross pushed the latch on the iron gate. It failed to move. *Locked?* She looked at it. *Locked!* She rattled the gate. A hollow clanging echoed through the garden.

Presently, there came a slow slap-slap of sandals down the curving red brick walk. A calf-eyed serving girl in a wrinkled brown dress emerged from the greenery, stopped on the other side of the gate. There was a look of sleepy insolence on her face.

"Good afternoon, Señora."

"Why is this gate locked?" demanded Mrs. Ross. "I wish to see Don Jaime at once."

"Don Jaime?" The girl shrugged. "El Presidente makes for himself a visit to Mexico City."

Mrs. Ross stiffened. "To Mexico? When does he return?" She felt furious with the girl, those staring eyes.

"Who knows?" Another shrug lifted the brown shoulders. "He is gone in the automobile to transport el Señor Hoblitt to Mexico City. He has not informed me when he returns."

With Hoblitt! Mrs. Ross maintained self-control at the cost of great effort. "But did he not say where they were going?"

"To Mexico City, Señora." The girl nodded, made as if to return to the house. "*Buenas tardes …*"

"*Buenas tardes,*" murmured Mrs. Ross. She turned away, heard the serving girl's footsteps recede toward the house.

To Mexico City with Hoblitt! All that fool Jaime has to do is drop one word about Paulita's condition! One careless word! She felt that she sat on a bomb with the fuse already burning. *And Hoblitt told Paulita that he's coming back!*

Mrs. Ross's feet began moving automatically in the direction of her house. *Maybe I could take Paulita away to some … But, no. She wouldn't leave now.* Mrs. Ross mumbled to herself, discarded plan after plan. *A hired guard? No. Costly. And Mexican watchmen are notoriously lax. A call to the Turismo in Mexico City? But what could I say?*

Her stumbling, distracted progress caught immediate attention in San Juan. Several villagers tried to stop her, help her. She shook them off.

A small boy was sent running for the doctor: "The Señora Ross is sick from the sun!"

In this manner, Mrs. Ross came to the corner on her own street, saw Dr. Herrera striding toward her, Serena standing beyond him at the gate.

"Here now, what's this?" demanded the doctor. His square-jowled face showed concern as he took Mrs. Ross's arm, helped her along the walk.

"Let go of me!" ordered Mrs. Ross. The doctor only gripped her arm tighter.

Serena held the gate open, stood to one side as they approached. Her flat face was firm in its indignation. "I told her not to go out. But, oh, no; she insisted."

"I'm perfectly all right," said Mrs. Ross.

"She forced me," said Serena. "Yes! She forced me to get her things. And now: look!"

Mrs. Ross focused her attention on the doctor. There was a Merthiolate stain on his shirtfront. "I'm perfectly all right," she repeated.

But she stumbled on the first step up to her porch, experienced a wave of dizziness. *Good Lord!* she thought. *Maybe I'm really getting sick!* Dr. Herrera's hand felt comforting as he steadied her.

"One is not as young as one once was," he said.

"That's what I told her." Serena brushed past, clattered on ahead, lifting her skirts out of the way as she climbed. "I told her that very thing."

Perhaps it was a suggestion, or all the walking around after the days in bed, or a retreat from reality … or even a germ. Mrs. Ross found herself in her own bed with a fever that climbed higher and higher as night fell over San Juan.

She lay back on the perspiration-soggy sheet, stared at the *ropero* beyond the foot of her bed. It stood there in its tall, carved mahogany splendor with the mirrors on its doors glistening, and it grew more and more alive as the darkness deepened. She told herself that it was just the place where she hung her clothing, a piece of furniture, a sort of closet. But the thing grew faces and arms in the darkness. And when the neon cross atop the church a block away was lighted, the mirrors picked up reflections of it that were shattered by the blinds.

The *ropero* glared at her with purple eyes.

Mrs. Ross twisted against the clinging sheet. It was so hot. She searched for strength to throw off the cover, failed. So hot. Her head felt light, whirling. The night, the fever—everything grew indistinct, rambling. People moved about. Lights flickered. The purple eyes glared.

It was all a great incoherency.

For a while, Mrs. Ross thought she was back in the northland. There was a strong impression of her old entrance hall with its red velvet draperies and the smell of the oil heaters in everything and the sound of the girls squabbling somewhere. She imagined she could hear the clapboards creaking in a cold snap, felt the old, never-forgotten chill and thought: *I didn't make it away to the sunshine. It was all a dream. I never made it.*

And there was a girl who stayed right there—right in the shadowy flickering beside the bed. It was Gertie, but not Gertie. The face and hair were more like Serena's. Still, the voice echoing in Mrs. Ross's head could not be mistaken: Gertie's voice. The woman kept chanting: *"Men are all alike. Men are all alike. Men are all alike. Men are …"*

Mrs. Ross thought she would go mad with the repetition. She muttered in English: "Make her go away. Make her stop that."

Serena, seated at the bedside in the light of a single candle (there had been another failure of the "generation"), heard the unintelligible English, leaned forward. She pressed a damp cloth to Mrs. Ross's head as Dr. Herrera had instructed. The aged skin looked dry, leathery.

"Pobrecita," whispered Serena. *Poor little one.*

A tear ran down Serena's right cheek, fell onto the single white sheet covering her employer. The tear left a round mark that faded quickly in the heat. Abruptly, the candle guttered, dimmed. It took several heartbeats for the light to resume its yellow wavering.

Serena had tensed, every muscle frozen while the light flickered.

Now, she took a quavering breath, crossed herself. (Everyone is San Juan knew it made the most terrible danger for a lone candle to go out beside a sickbed.) She gathered her nerve, scurried out into the dark house, returned with a handful of fresh candles and saucers to hold the candles. Only when they were burning securely all around the room did she resume her seat.

Toward midnight the fever broke. Mrs. Ross drifted into a deep, dreamless sleep. Serena curled up on the serape rug beside the bed, there to stir upright every time Mrs. Ross shifted. Twice, Serena arose to replace candles.

In the morning, word went from doorway to doorway around San Juan: "Mrs. Ross still lives. Her fever is gone, but she is very weak."

Paulita sent her aunt to the church to light a candle before the Virgin. A number of candles were being burned there for Mrs. Ross. She was close-fisted, rich, sharp-tongued, and a Protestant. But most agreed she was fair. And being close-fisted was a virtue of sorts— admired, at least. And she had made many jobs in San Juan, and there was all that time she had spent helping Paulita.

Beneath the concern lay the unvocalized feeling that they would hate to lose *any* village "institution."

Even those few who did not like Mrs. Ross said: "Better the devil you know that the devil you don't."

And the procession of herbal remedies resumed.

Convalescence fell into a slow, orderly ritual. The sudden attack of fever had frightened Mrs. Ross more than she cared to admit. She ate the broths Serena prepared, took Dr. Herrera's pills, even sampled the Jamaica tea. The tea was sickly sweet and astringent, left her mouth with an alum pucker. Its dregs killed the potted begonia on the windowsill beside her bed.

The death of the plant was interpreted as a very bad omen by Serena until she reflected that sometimes these things went by opposites, the flower being taken in place of the human.

Don Jaime returned on the afternoon of the fourth day after the fever. Passage of his long black Buick was noted even behind doors in the village by the familiar squeaks and the thumps of its tires on the cobblestones. He called on Mrs. Ross within the hour, bringing a basketful of purple-spotted orchids from the *jardín de vidreo* at Jocotepec. But Dr. Herrera had barred all visitors, even one who was a very old friend (and possibly even closer than that if one believed the stories).

The orchids were sent in with Serena, accompanied by a sealed note that, while a good example of Latin overstatement, failed to say anything about the mysterious trip to Mexico City with Hoblitt.

"San Juan is prostrate with grief at your illness, and I am the most grief-stricken of all," he wrote. "Make haste to bring the sunshine of your health back to our hearts." He signed it: "Your devoted servant," and then the official touch, "D. Jaime Cervelles y Madera, El Presidente de San Juan."

No one could ever get Jaime to sign himself any other way, Mrs. Ross reflected. She dropped the note onto her bed stand, thinking wryly that Serena certainly would make the opportunity to read it and report its contents.

A wasp climbed over the orchids that Serena had enshrined on a small table brought in from the hall and placed at the foot of the bed in front of the *ropera*. Mrs. Ross prudently kept her attention on the wasp as it lifted itself, circled the room, buzzed out the open door.

From outside there came the *clop-clop* of a burro train passing: quick-footed and light, a sure indication they were empty. A thin trail of charcoal smoke hung on the bedroom air: a sign that evening meals were being prepared in the neighborhood.

Mrs. Ross wished she could have talked to Don Jaime. But she *did* feel weak, and it was so much trouble to argue with Serena. Lassitude hung like a fog around Mrs. Ross.

The Hoblitt problem will have to wait, she thought. *Jaime knows the danger. I've done everything I can.* She sighed. *I cannot be responsible for such things when I'm this ill.*

And a small prayer hovered just behind her lips: "Please don't let anything happen to Paulita."

Serena came in from the hall with a green cup containing broth. She still wore the bandage over her burned finger, although the gauze had been grimed by various juices and sauces from the kitchen. Her brown dress hung sack-like, with stains on it marking the day's activities: a teardrop of tomato pulp on the breast, a grease spot at the belt line and again near the hem, a smudge of whitewash on the left shoulder where she had rubbed against a wall.

Mrs. Ross blinked at the sight. The woman just let herself go when there was no one around to keep after her!

Serena's face wore its brave-in-the-face-of-doom smile. She held out the cup. "Chicken broth, Señora. It makes the strength to return."

Mrs. Ross accepted the cup, blew at the steam curling from the liquid surface.

"You must drink it hot," said Serena.

Anger gave Mrs. Ross a surge of strength. "I'm not going to scald myself!" She held the cup gingerly. Even the handle felt hot. "Have you heard anything about Hoblitt?"

Serena straightened a fold of the bed covers. "He is gone, Señora."

"I guess you won't get to pose for him after all," said Mrs. Ross. She watched Serena's face for reaction.

Serena shrugged. "As you said: artists are fickle. Now, drink the broth."

"What is happening around the village?"

"Dr. Herrera says I am not to gossip with you. It wastes your strength. Drink the broth. It will soon be time for your medicine."

"Your dress is a sight," said Mrs. Ross. "You've spilled things all over it."

Serena spoke through stiff lips: "It makes very much more work when someone is ill! There is no time left for me to do things for myself."

"Have you been watering my plants?"

"Everything is cared for, Señora. No evil befalls. Now drink the broth."

"Did Dr. Herrera tell you when I could have visitors?"

"When you are stronger, not before. Please drink the broth. You must drink it hot."

"I wish to see Don Jaime as soon as …"

"Señora! The broth. Please?"

Mrs. Ross could feel her false strength fading. She sipped the liquid, found its temperature just bearable. The chicken flavor covered something faintly aromatic—a distant flower pungency. She mentally shrugged, downed the broth.

Best not to ask, she thought.

Serena smiled benignly, took the cup, *slap-slapped* out of the room.

CHAPTER 10

On a Tuesday morning, eight days after the fever, Mrs. Ross donned a blue housecoat, ventured out of bed for the first time since her illness. Dr. Herrera had said she could get up tomorrow, but she felt impatience growing as her strength returned. And it was so degrading—this being *really* ill—all the intimate attentions that had to be turned over to another human. She looked down beside the bed for her slippers. They were gone. Serena had kicked them underneath the bed again.

The maid could be heard working downstairs: a rattle of pans, the quick patter of sandals. Tantalizing odors of food drifted into the bedroom.

Mrs. Ross grasped a corner of her bed's headboard to steady herself, shuffled to the window, raised the blinds all the way. She sensed that it was a symbolic act. Her knees felt rubbery, but it was a delicious sensation to stand there, feeling the sunshine pour across her body.

A shiver passed through her as she remembered the delirium. *I did make it to the sunshine,* she thought.

Serena had replaced the potted begonia on the windowsill. The new plant appeared sickly, claw branches reaching toward the outside and with only a scattering of pale green serrated leaves. Mrs. Ross couldn't classify it.

I must ask Serena what this plant is, she thought.

She looked past the plant to the lake. Toward the near shore the water held a deep ultramarine tone shading to cobalt. But farther out, the color faded into grey, then white—reflecting a fleecy billow of cumulus clouds piled over the distant hills: the first storm gathering of the season.

It'll be raining soon, she thought. *I must get Serena to bring my herbs in from the balcony after the first showers or they'll be drowned.* She took a deep breath of the warm, muggy air, thought: *I'll have Jaime in tomorrow to find out about Hoblitt. Doubtless there's some simple explanation. Most likely Hoblitt had no money, and Jaime—being soft in the heart as well as the head—personally escorted him out of town. It'd be just like Jaime.*

The thought amused her.

And I must check my herbs to make sure Serena has been giving them proper care. You have to keep after her every second to get things done.

Mrs. Ross crept back across the serape rug, enjoying the rough wool under her bare feet. She turned, sank onto the bed. Sunlight threw a golden pattern across the blue housecoat. She pulled up the garment, drank in the sensation of warmth on her knees.

Tomorrow I will sit on the balcony for a while, she thought. *It'll be good to talk to Paulita.* And she told herself: *The girl will be a little sad, no doubt, when Hoblitt doesn't return. Maybe this will teach her a lesson.*

But the next morning when Mrs. Ross opened the French doors and looked down through the openwork of the balcony, Paulita's window stood closed, empty. The barred iron shutters had been pulled together, and Mrs. Ross could see the edge of the big padlock where they joined. Shards of plaster lay on the sidewall from a freshly cracked place on the wall beside the window. Raw adobe showed where the plaster had been.

No one has swept, thought Mrs. Ross.

There came a sudden roll of thunder from across the lake. Mrs. Ross felt a constriction in her chest, thought: *Could anything have happened to Paulita?*

She turned, stumbled back into the house, calling: "Serena! Serena!"

There came a clatter of sandaled feet pounding up the back stairs. Serena burst through the swinging doors beside the sideboard. Her face was all staring eyes as she stepped just inside the room. She was panting with exertion. One long braid hung forward over her breast.

The door slapped to stillness behind her.

"Where is Paulita?"

"Oh …" Serena took a deep breath, steadied herself with a hand on the corner of the sideboard. "The way you called … I thought …"

"Has something happened to Paulita?" screamed Mrs. Ross.

"I did not tell you. The doctor said I was not to spend so much time gossiping."

Mrs. Ross fought down panic. "What has happened?"

"It is nothing bad, Señora. They have taken Paulita to Guadalajara to fit her with braces on the legs. Don Jaime himself has taken them in his automobile. Paulita will be able to walk a little easier. Is that not a good thing?"

Mrs. Ross exhaled in relief, took a moment to regain her composure, then thought: *Braces. Why didn't I ever think of that?*

She said: "When does Paulita return?"

"They said on Saturday, Señora."

And Mrs. Ross thought: *I wonder where they got the money for such a thing?* She knew that the Romera family existed on a small pension and infrequent checks sent by an uncle who ran a charter boat in Veracruz. *Perhaps they have been saving for this,* she thought.

"Well, don't just stand there," said Mrs. Ross. "My plants need watering. You've been ignoring them."

"Señora!" Serena's round face stiffened with outrage. "Every day I carried the big watering can out there and cared for your plants. Every day! Not once did I …"

"Then get about it!"

Mrs. Ross turned away, shuffled toward her bedroom. She realized she was being unfair. The herbs looked as healthy and lush as they ever had. *But there must be something she's let slide,* she thought. *I'll find it as soon as I can get around better.*

Saturday morning Mrs. Ross felt almost her old self. She got out of bed debating whether to give the house a thorough inspection or to hire the village taxi for a tour of her tenant properties. She opened the *ropero*, studied the ranks of her clothing, chose a gray dress with emerald piping at the collar and sleeves.

A swaying string of cobweb that dipped from the top of the *ropero* to the wall caught Mrs. Ross's eye. She frowned.

The house comes first, she decided. *If it's anything like this room it must be a shambles!*

There were voices outside by the front gate. Mrs. Ross slipped into the grey dress, buttoned it, listening: *Serena with a tradesman.* A squawking chicken raised a hubbub somewhere down the street, set the dogs to barking.

Serena finished her bargaining. Mrs. Ross adjusted the belt of her dress, heard a burro driver call to his animal, the abrupt rhythm of hooves on cobblestones.

Downstairs, a door closed with a heavy thump.

Mrs. Ross left her bedroom, crossed the hall to the upstairs sitting room, thence to the red-draped French doors. The odor of her potted herbs hung heavily there. She pulled back a corner of the draperies, peered down through the balcony railing.

Paulita sat at her window, black braids tied with red bows. Morning sunshine poured in on her, washed her cheeks with golden light. The Hidalgo beauty stood out strongly in Paulita this morning: proud curve of neck, a tiny smile on the passionate lips, the flashing dark eyes.

Mrs. Ross smiled. *Everything will be as it was.*

Paulita was knitting on something green this morning. Her fingers flew across the work with a sharp rhythm.

I'll just say hello, thought Mrs. Ross. She opened the doors, stepped outside, leaned across the riotous green of the parsley.

It was then that Mrs. Ross noticed Paulita's self-conscious attention to the knitting, the way she avoided looking up when it was obvious that she must have heard the French doors.

Mrs. Ross became aware of a noise beneath her balcony, looked down.

Hoblitt!

He was bent over his sketch pad. The duck curl of blond hair pointed upward at the nape of his neck.

Mrs. Ross had the sensation that time had slipped backward, that she had lived through this moment before. Then a sense of horrible fascination overcame her as she realized that Hoblitt was not sketching, but was using the pad to conceal something from Paulita. Sunlight glistened off nickel-plated metal. Mrs. Ross could not quite see what it was he held in his hand, but her mind leaped to its own conclusion: *He has a gun! Good heavens! He's found out about Paulita's legs!*

She did the only thing she could think of—pushed the pottery container of parsley off the rail directly onto Hoblitt, turned and raced downstairs as fast as her legs would carry her.

Paulita was gone from the window when Mrs. Ross reached the street. Hoblitt lay face up, diagonally across the sidewalk. His chest rose and fell unevenly. Dirt and bits of greenery had spattered his shirt, mostly on the left side where the heavy pottery box had struck his shoulder. The force of the blow had hurled him almost to the gutter. There was a pale, defenseless look to his craggy face. His lips appeared bloodless.

Mrs. Ross put her left hand to her cheek. *I must do something,* she thought. *A boy! I must send a boy for the doctor!*

Several youngsters already were gathering at the intersection beyond Hoblitt. They bunched together as though for protection, presented a mass of dark, tousled hair and faded, wrong-sized clothing. Mrs. Ross recognized Antonio Muñez among them, called out: "Antonio! Run get Doctor Herrera!"

"Tanis already has gone," said Antonio.

The boys inched toward her, moving in a body, their attention focused on Hoblitt. "He is not yet dead," said one. "See, his chest moves."

Mrs. Ross heard a door open, glanced across the cobblestones at the Romera house. Paulita stood in the doorway on her crutches. Light gleamed along the new metal braces supporting her legs. A look of fury contorted her features. She tried to push forward, but was held back by her aunt.

As Mrs. Ross watched, the aunt led Paulita back into the shadows of the house. The door was closed, presenting its worn boards to the street.

There came the sound of the bolt being secured.

She saw me push the box! thought Mrs. Ross. *She must have turned while I was looking at Hoblitt.*

Piping whistles sounded from around the corner. The police came: a pack of tan uniforms and black shoes that thumped along the sidewalk. One carried a stretcher on his shoulder, the canvas laces flying loose behind him.

Dr. Herrera trotted along behind, black bag swinging from one long arm. He looked like a great lumbering football player.

Police Chief Beto, Don Jaime's nephew, brought up the rear, mustaches flapping, his fat body vibrating.

"Do not crowd too closely to the body!" he called.

Dr. Herrera put down his bag, knelt beside Hoblitt, concealing the fallen man's head and shoulders from Mrs. Ross. The police ignored Chief Beto's order, pressed closely about the doctor. They presented a tan wall to Mrs. Ross. The children scattered around the group, peering between legs, past belts.

There was a rattling of iron at the gate behind Mrs. Ross. She glanced back, saw Serena standing there. Mrs. Ross recognized the vacant look on her maid's face: the prophetess-of-doom expression. Serena was recalling all the omens that had warned of disaster.

"A broken collar bone," said Dr. Herrera.

Mrs. Ross returned her attention to the pack of tan backs, the doctor's squatting figure. Movement of the group opened a gap through which she saw Hoblitt's belt, a strip of soiled white shirt.

"He is unconscious, but he should live," said Dr. Herrera. "Someone bring me three pieces of wood about so long, so thick." He gestured with his hands. "I must immobilize this before he can be moved."

A small boy was sent running.

Chief Beto detached himself from the group, stepped up to Mrs. Ross. He touched his mustache deferentially. "A terrible thing, this, Señora." His shoe-button eyes pinned her.

Mrs. Ross thought: *What a hateful, stupid little man.*

"If you would be so kind," said Beto. He cleared his throat. "How did this happen?"

Mrs. Ross focused on a spot of egg yolk staining the man's tan shirtfront. "I stumbled against the box on my balcony. He was standing directly beneath."

"What a destructive conspiracy of events." Beto shook his head. "You stumbled. No doubt you are still weak from your recent illness."

"It was careless of me," murmured Mrs. Ross. She felt bits of her courage returning.

"But you must not blame yourself," protested Beto. "God may use anyone as an instrument of tragedy."

The other policemen had turned their attention to her. "Truly spoken," agreed one.

"He has seen the reason of this thing," said another.

And Mrs. Ross thought: *Yes-men are the same the world over.* She was beginning to be thankful for Beto's limited intelligence.

Dr. Herrera straightened, brushed dirt from his hands. He glanced back at Mrs. Ross. She avoided his eyes, looked across at the Romera home where motion had caught her attention. The aunt was closing Paulita's window. A protesting screech sounded from the frame.

Presently, the boy returned with the three lengths of board.

"Ah, good," said Dr. Herrera. He pressed copper coins into the boy's hand, took the wood. Again, he knelt beside Hoblitt. "Perhaps we can set this right here while he is unconscious. You." He motioned to one of the police. "Hold him like this."

"What're y' doin'?" It was Hoblitt speaking in English, his voice faint and reedy. "Ooooooo!"

Dr. Herrera said: "Mrs. Ross, would you do me the favor of telling the young man that we only desire to help him, that he must remain quiet?"

Beto moved aside. The other police made room for her. Mrs. Ross stepped across shards of pottery, clumps of dirt, bent beside the doctor. As she moved, she made a quick search of the scene, looking for Hoblitt's weapon. *It could be anywhere in this mess,* she thought.

"You must speak loudly," said Dr. Herrera.

"Young man!" said Mrs. Ross. And she thought: *I must be the one to find the weapon and secrete it. We must dispose of this without scandal.*

Hoblitt groaned. His eyelids flickered.

"Young man!" repeated Mrs. Ross. "You have a broken collar bone, young man. You must remain quiet while the doctor takes care of it!"

Hoblitt gritted his teeth. Abruptly, his eyes snapped open. He glared up at Mrs. Ross. "Well, if it isn't Kodiak Kate!"

Mrs. Ross shot bolt upright with shock. *That hideous name! He knows!*

"You didn't quite get me, did you?" rasped Hoblitt. He clenched his teeth as Dr. Herrera cut away the shirt, exposed a chest covered by blond hair, a muscular arm. There was a mottled blue area spreading along the corded line of his shoulder.

Mrs. Ross put a hand to her cheek.

"Have to give you credit for trying, though!" panted Hoblitt.

Mrs. Ross's lips worked, but no sound came. All she could think was: *God in heaven! He knows! He knows!* And then: *Thank God these others speak no English.* She shot a glance at the Romera house, saw its blank, sealed face.

Hoblitt arched his head backward in anguish as Dr. Herrera began taping a board across the shoulders. Mrs. Ross gulped, felt a pang of remorse.

The artist gasped, took a deep breath, stared at Mrs. Ross. "You're going to pay for this!"

"Of course I'll pay for it," whispered Mrs. Ross. She cleared her throat, spoke louder. "It'll all go on my bill." And she thought: *What if he tells? How they'd laugh here in San Juan!*

"That's not what I mean," said Hoblitt.

Dr. Herrera smoothed a last length of surgical tape into place across Hoblitt's chest, stood up, spoke to Mrs. Ross. "I am going to administer a sedative. Will you ask the young man first about his family, whom to notify, which hospital he would prefer?"

Mrs. Ross found momentary difficulty in shifting back to Spanish. She swallowed, said: "I will take care of all expenses."

"What's he saying?" demanded Hoblitt.

The anger of desperation overcame Mrs. Ross. She squatted beside Hoblitt, demanded: "How did you find out about me? Who else knows?" And she thought: *Does Serena know? Jaime? Is this what they really gossip about?*

Hoblitt gritted his teeth. Perspiration stood out along his forehead. "Can't he give me something to stop the pain?"

"He is preparing something," said Mrs. Ross. "How long have you known?"

"At the art show in Mexico City," whispered Hoblitt. He squinted, wet his lips with his tongue. "I showed a portrait of you—the one Don Jaime had me make for him—only I changed it the way he wanted: made you look younger."

Mrs. Ross put a hand to her throat. "Like the sketch you sent me?"

"Yeah."

Just as I feared. Oh, why didn't I do something then? Through dry lips she said: "Who saw the picture?"

"Tourist," panted Hoblitt. "Old guy. Named John Sullivan." He subsided, breathing in shallow gasps.

Old John! thought Mrs. Ross. *God in heaven!*

She said: "What did he tell you?"

Hoblitt's lips trembled.

Behind Mrs. Ross, Dr. Herrera said: "Please do not take too long, Señora."

Mrs. Ross ignored the interruption, hardly heard it. "Did you tell this tourist where I live?"

"Wish I had," whispered Hoblitt. "But after he told me who the portrait looked like ... I told him you were ... dead ... you died years ago. He wanted to buy the picture, but Don Jaime wouldn't sell."

"Did you tell Don Jaime what the man said?" asked Mrs. Ross.

Recognizing the name, Dr. Herrera said: "Don Jaime has already been summoned, Señora."

Hoblitt said: "I didn't tell anyone."

"What ... did Sullivan say to you?" she whispered.

Hoblitt held his head rigid, turned his eyes, stared directly at her. There was sharp clarity in his attention, and his voice came out strongly: "He said my portrait was the spitting image of Kodiak Kate, who used to run the best house in Juneau. He said you were the smartest business woman he ever met: everything in your house was for sale ... except Kate herself. That's what he told me!"

Dr. Herrera cleared his throat. "Do you have the necessary information, Señora?"

Mrs. Ross answered without turning: "One moment, Doctor." She shifted back to English, attention fixed on Hoblitt. "What do you intend to do with this information?"

Hoblitt spoke in a low, musing voice. "Been thinking. At first I wasn't going to do anything. But since ..." He swallowed, and a muscle rippled along his chest. "What'd you hit me with?"

"A flower box fell off my balcony," said Mrs. Ross.

"Fell!" grated Hoblitt. His attention wavered past her, came back. "What happened to that thing I was carrying?"

Mrs. Ross had lost all contact with her previous suspicions. "What thing?" she asked.

"Model. Little wheelchair. Sold portrait of Paulita. Sent part back with Don Jaime ... braces ... her legs. Rest ... money for wheelchair. Making special one." He blinked, focused on Mrs. Ross. "I was nerving myself to take the model over to Miss Romera when ..." He closed his eyes, fell silent.

Dr. Herrera bent beside Mrs. Ross. "I must administer the sedative now. It is not good to leave him thus." He swabbed a Merthiolate-odorous daub of cotton across Hoblitt's bare arm. A red smear appeared on the flesh behind the cotton.

Mrs. Ross could not take her attention from Hoblitt's face. *What a fool I've been!* she thought. She said: "What are you going to do, Mr. Hoblitt?"

The artist opened his eyes, swallowed convulsively as Dr. Herrera sank the hypodermic needle into his arm, depressed the plunger. Presently Hoblitt began speaking in a low voice: "In the old days artists had their patrons. You're going to become a patron of the arts." He stared at her, a cold, commanding expression. "Right here in San Juan. You're going to support a starving young artist. Won't cost you much. Couple thousand a year. Give me time to paint what I want … like those portraits." He cleared his throat, attention yawing across her face. "What'd he give me? Feel woozy."

He's going to blackmail me! thought Mrs. Ross.

Hoblitt found a reserve of consciousness, held his gaze on her face. "Not gonna walk under your balcony ever again!"

"That was an accident," murmured Mrs. Ross. And she thought: *He's going to blackmail me for the rest of my life!*

Dr. Herrera lowered one ham-like hand, pulled her upright—gently, firmly. "We must put him on the stretcher now." He patted her shoulder. "Do not feel too badly. The bones will heal."

Hoblitt stared up at Mrs. Ross, eyes, glazing from the narcotics. "Tell y' somethin' else," he slurred. "Gonna marry tha' g'l across' street!" He summoned inner reserves, "Don't care what you or her crazy aunt think!" He fell silent while Dr. Herrera and the police shifted him onto the stretcher. Bits of dirt fell off his trousers onto the cobblestones. Then, "All y'r dough! Never gettin' her a wheelchair!"

Mrs. Ross watched the police carry the stretcher up the sidewalk, around the corner. Dr. Herrera remained standing beside her. "Which hospital, Señora?"

"The Foreign Clinic in Guadalajara," murmured Mrs. Ross. "Specialists should be called in, if you believe it advisable. See that he has the best of care. Anything he requires."

Her mind was resuming its usual alertness. She thought: *Blackmail? He'll see. I've never met the man yet I couldn't beat in a deal.* She squinted. *He sold the portrait of Paulita. And Jaime bought the one of me. That means the work is marketable. Given proper handling, he can get top prices.* She began mentally calculating how much commission she could charge. And part of her mind started working out a plan to get her portrait away from Don Jaime.

Dr. Herrera cleared his throat.

But Mrs. Ross's attention was lost in her plans. *Can't let Hoblitt enter any more mixed shows,* she thought. *Divides attention too much. He'll need some one-man shows, good advance publicity.* She nodded to herself. *This could become quite profitable—much better than a couple thousand a year just in commissions.* She suppressed a smile at the thought of self-supporting blackmail.

Another idea struck Mrs. Ross. She turned to face Dr. Herrera, who was studying her with a puzzled frown.

"You feel all right, Señora?"

"Perfectly all right," she assured him. "How long before the young man will be able to resume his painting?"

"How *simpático!*" blurted Dr. Herrera. He shook his head in wonder at this magnificent woman whose thoughts were only for the young man injured in the regrettable accident.

"How long?" demanded Mrs. Ross.

"It is the left shoulder," said Dr. Herrera. "He paints with the right hand, does he not?" The doctor nodded. "He should be up and around in a week or so. Wearing a cast, of course."

"Good!"

And Mrs. Ross thought wryly: *Well, it won't be the first time I've sold beauty!*

"Perhaps you should go inside and rest for a while," said Dr. Herrera. "Your illness ..."

"I'm fully recovered," said Mrs. Ross. "You run along now and take care of that young man. There must be no complications. See that he gets everything he requires. And put it all on my bill."

"Well ... if you're sure you feel all right," said Dr. Herrera. "But do not stand too long in the sun of noonday. And call me immediately if you feel dizzy, eh?

Or any pains of the stomach?"

"I will call you, Doctor."

"I'm sure you will." He executed a little bow, gave her his English notice of departure: "Goodbye now."

Mrs. Ross watched until he rounded the corner. A shudder passed through her. *I might have killed that young man!* she thought. And there was in the thought a touch of the same feeling she experienced at the possibility of waste or mishandling in any of her financial empire. She took a deep, relieved breath. *Well … this will shake down in time.*

A metallic gleam in the dirt at her feet caught Mrs. Ross's attention. She stopped, removed a crude model wheelchair from a hole left by a missing cobblestone. The model appeared undamaged, preserved from trampling feet by the hole in which it had lodged. She shook off the debris of parsley and dirt that had partially concealed it, stared at the model: a pathetic little thing, the kind used in window displays.

How can I face Paulita? she wondered. *After what she saw.*

Mrs. Ross glanced across the street where both door and window remained closed, bolted. She felt old, ashamed: the shame much more involved in Hoblitt's indictment of her than in her error of judgment about the artist.

I've been an old fool, she thought. Then: *Well … we're never too old to learn.*

Don Jaime's lank form skirted the corner ahead of Mrs. Ross. The mayor bore down on her almost at a trot.

His narrow face was drawn downward in a look of dog-eyed melancholy. His severe black suit looked just a little disheveled. He pulled up in front of Mrs. Ross, wiped perspiration from his forehead with a white handkerchief which he returned to a side pocket.

"Good morning, Jaime," said Mrs. Ross.

"Emma," pleaded Don Jaime. "What have you done?"

"It was an accident," said Mrs. Ross. She felt stirrings of anger at Don Jaime, thought: *Why does he have to intrude just now?*

"Aiiii!" wailed Don Jaime. "Another accident!" He stretched out both hands, palms up. "Emma, I asked you not to do this! I knew in my heart the young man was harmless. From the moment I first began dealing with him, I knew he was a good young man, very sympathetic, very …"

"Jaime, please," she said. "Not now."

"There will be another letter from the Turismo," he accused. "And what can I tell them?"

Mrs. Ross took a deep breath, hefted the model in her hand. *I'll have Serena wash this off before I take it over,* she thought. *Yes! And I will tell Paulita what Hoblitt said about marrying her! That will take her mind off anything else.*

She felt the entire situation settling into place. And abrupt insight struck her as she recalled what Hoblitt's painting had revealed about Paulita: the latent coldness, the cruelty, the pride. Serve him right if he does marry her!

"What am I to tell Turismo?" insisted Don Jaime. He wrung his thin hands.

Mrs. Ross half turned away, stopped, looked back at the mayor. *To think that I could have married him once,* she thought. *God watches over women and fools.*

Inspiration filled Mrs. Ross. "Tell Turismo," she said, "… tell them that San Juan is the fairest flower in all of Mexico's tourist attractions. But tell them that every such blossom must have around it a bush of thorns. Everything of beauty must have at least one flaw in it. Otherwise people do not realize how beautiful it truly is. That is what you must tell them. Tell them that I—Emma Ross—I am the thorn in San Juan. Tell them that!"

And she reflected: *How right I am! And now I'm saddled with that artist. What a complicated thorn!* She mentally shrugged, thought: *Well … anyway, I still have the sunshine.*

A roll of thunder crashed from across the lake.

Looking toward the noise, Mrs. Ross saw a line squall moving toward her over the darkening water like a black wall.

"Good day to you," she said to Don Jaime, who still stood there staring at her, his brows furrowed in puzzlement.

Then, she hurried inside before the rain struck.

About the Author

FRANK HERBERT (1920–1986) created the most beloved novel in the annals of science fiction, *Dune*. He was a man of many facets, of countless passageways that ran through an intricate mind. His magnum opus is a reflection of this, a classic work that stands as one of the most complex, multi-layered novels ever written in any genre. Today the novel is more popular than ever, with new readers continually discovering it and telling their friends to pick up a copy. It has been translated into dozens of languages and has sold almost 20 million copies.

Herbert wrote more than twenty other novels, including *Hellstrom's Hive*, *The White Plague*, *The Green Brain*, and *The Dosadi Experiment*. During his life, he received great acclaim for his sweeping vision and the deep philosophical underpinnings in his writings. His life is detailed in the Hugo-nominated biography *Dreamer of Dune*, by Brian Herbert.

92

Other Unpublished Frank Herbert Novels from WordFire Press

WordFire Press has produced three other never-before-published novels written by Frank Herbert, *High-Opp*, *Angels' Fall*, and *A Game of Authors*.

Please enjoy the following sample first chapters.

Angels' Fall

Angels' Fall is a gripping thriller set in the South American jungles. After a plane crash deep in the Amazon, freelance pilot Jeb Logan has to keep himself and his passengers alive in a gruelling trip down-river. Adrift in the wreckage of the plane with Jeb are a beautiful singer, her young son, and a ruthless murderer clinging to the last thread of sanity.

With supplies running out and nature itself turning against them, this small desperate group struggles to survive against the jungle—and each other.

Sample Chapter

In that stealthy moment just before awakening, a nightmare invaded Jeb Logan's mind. It implanted an empty feeling that became—at the actual moment of awakening—a premonition.

And that set the pattern for the day.

It was a slow day starting. The first black clouds of the Ecuadorian wet season delayed the dawn. Daylight came somnolently out of darkness like a woman stirring beside her lover. Then the morning wind herded the clouds eastward toward the jungle.

But there was still no rain, and a dusty haze shrouded the dry highlands. It gave the sky the color of sifting ashes.

Sunlight flattened out in a few mica brilliants against the eastern edge of the Andean foothill town where Logan lived. The town was called Milagro after a local miracle, a legend recounted innumerable times: A young boy suffering from a jungle fever had awakened from a deep dream of his own and staggered into the dusty streets. Pointing to the sky, he shouted in Spanish, "See the angels! See the angels!"

The villagers had stared, and the little boy collapsed, sweating, burning. Some of the watchers thought they might have seen angels, too, up in the sky. The fever had already taken many of the people, and yet this boy miraculously recovered. He claimed that as he slept, shivered, sweated, all the while he had been with the angels. *Milagro.* Miracle.

In Jeb's own dream, a much darker dream, he had seen angels too. Great, soaring, heavenly creatures with pearlescent wings, surrounded by a halo-glow that was part humidity in the air and part the shine of a heavenly deity. In his dream they had been watching over him, soaring ahead as Jeb made his own way on a quest through the jungle, winding and curving on a course that made sense only with dream-logic. His path was twisted, unpredictable, and when he made the wrong choice and took an incorrect turn, the angels did not bless him for his independence. Rather, they reeled, struggled to attain heaven, and instead they tumbled, falling from the sky.

In the nightmare, Jeb had watched, felt the warning, the premonition. Yet he continued. This was his quest, not one determined by the angels of Milagro or anywhere else.

He had a journey to make.

He met a boat down at Puerto Bolivar. He had still been hypnotized by the mystery and the hothouse odor of the jungle above the coastal town. A luminous-eyed man all in white had squatted in the thick shade of the corrugated iron customs building, singing to the tune picked out on a pearl-inlaid guitar:

"Give me a while longer, death —
Stay your hand while my river flows on.
I do not yet want your dark sea.
For I have a love with grey smoke in her eyes,
And farewells are difficult for my tongue."

Jeb remembered his piecemeal translation of the song, stumbling through his rusty high school Spanish. Well, two years had changed that: now he could even dream the song in Spanish.

But the other details of his dream evaded him, driven away by the morning sounds. The futile questing of his mind left him troubled, unwilling to open his eyes: the first conscious touch of premonition.

Jeb stretched his leg muscles, felt the ripples of the single sheet that covered him. He was a long, knobby figure beneath the sheet: a moulding of angular shadows in soft focus under an olive drab canopy of mosquito netting. The weathered brown face protruding from one end of the sheet was angular, long: an Egyptian pharaoh's face with black hair peppered by grey at the temples.

"Well, what the hell," he muttered. "Time to get up."

He opened his eyes, blinked at a sudden memory: Hey! This the day that Bannon dame said she'd arrive! Well, by God! She's coming for nothing!

It had been a particularly frustrating telephone conversation. The long distance connection between Milagro and Puerto Bolivar had been dim and scratchy, and the woman at the other end full of Yankee determination.

"This is Mrs. Roger Bannon," she had said. "Are you the pilot?"

"Yes."

"What?"

"I said yes, I'm the pilot."

"We've never met, Mr. Logan. But you flew my husband and his partner to their rancho."

Then Jeb placed the name, recalled the husband: a scrawny little man with feverish eyes who'd hired Jeb to fly two men (Bannon and a partner named Gettler) to a jungle plantation on the Amazon watershed seven months before.

"What do you want, Mrs. Bannon?"

"I want to charter your plane for a flight to my husband's rancho."

"Sorry. No can do. My amphibian's dismantled for repairs."

"But the consul here says you have two planes!"

"Yes. But one's just a little single-engine float job."

"What kind of a boat?"

"Float! Mrs. Bannon. It won't do for that flight."

"But Roger's ranch is on a river!"

Here the connection had faded, and it had taken two full minutes to explain that he had too much liking for his skin to risk it by flying a single-engine floatplane over the Andes.

But she had persisted. "If it's a matter of money, Mr. Logan, I'm perfectly willing to …"

"No, dammit! It's not a matter of money! I'm just not …"

"We'll catch tomorrow afternoon's train, Mr. Logan. I'm sure we can work out something when …"

"Lady, you're wasting your time! Why don't you catch a mainline flight across to Belem and …?"

"I'll see you the day after tomorrow, Mr. Logan."

And by God! She'd hung up!

Jeb had jiggled the hook, gotten the operator with her impersonal, "*Bueno?*"

Now, he squirmed on his bed, dreading the encounter with Mrs. Bannon. He suspected that it would be a class-one scene. Such scenes always left him with a desire to get drunk and stay drunk for a week.

Jeb frowned, stared up through the netting at the veined cracks of the yellow-brown ceiling. During the night a green spider had set out its web from a shard of the plaster. Gossamer filaments stretched down to the framework that supported the mosquito net. Now, the spider waited with one foot delicately touching a trigger strand of its web. Jeb's attention shifted to a scorpion resting on the wall beside his bed from its night's hunt.

The "Ark! Ark!" cry of toucanets came from the dead tree outside his south wall. American jazz blared from the radio in the *aberote* across the road. The quick *pat pat-pat-pat-pat-pat* of his cook-maid, Maria, making tortillas sounded from the kitchen below. And there drifted past his nose the thin vapor-trail bite of burning chiles, scorched to remove the skin.

It was all infinitely familiar, and somehow poignant.

For a moment, Jeb lay quietly savoring the morning. Then his thoughts scalpeled the edge of an old memory that easy living had allowed him to evade for a long time: stark, snow-blanched Korean hills, his hands fighting the controls of a crippled B-26 as it skimmed between cold peaks ... and the bloody dead figure of Swede Parker, his co-pilot, in the other seat—a gale pouring through the bullet-shattered windshield. Jeb re-experienced the chill of that wind: another touch of the premonition.

Now, what the hell's got me on this morbid kick? he wondered. *That crazy Bannon dame insisting that I fly her inside! Well, I'll ...*

The pig in the courtyard emitted a scream like a frightened woman. Immediately, Maria's voice lifted in a string of curses that she did not know Jeb understood.

"Dump your droppings in my kitchen!" she screamed. "You son of a fat whore! You spawn of uncounted illegitimate ancestors! I'll boil your testicles!"

There came the clatter of a thrown pan.

Jeb chuckled, folded back the mosquito net. His movement disturbed the green spider on the ceiling. She darted onto her web, stopped, retreated. The scorpion curved up its tail, scurried into a crack in the wall.

From the courtyard came another pig squeal, the quick scuffling of Maria's footsteps. A water tin banged against the tiled edge of the reservoir outside the kitchen.

Jeb lifted his wristwatch from the chair beside the bed, slipped it on his wrist, glanced at the dial. *Eight thirty! What's happened to the morning?*

He swung his feet to the floor, rocked forward, stood up and stretched to his full six feet two inches. His left hand hitched his red and white striped shorts higher about his waist. A yellow robe hung on the wall at the head of the bed. He caught the robe in his right hand, gave it a casual shake to dislodge insects, draped it over his shoulders like a cape, and walked out onto the balcony.

"Maria!" he called.

Her voice came from a recess beneath him: "*Sí, señor?*" There was a slight quaver of age in the voice, but it sounded confident.

Jeb shifted his mental gears into Spanish: "Has there been a message from the airfield?"

Maria's replay was thick with the musical drawl of the altiplano Indians: "Manuelo sent to say that the airplane of two engines cannot yet be repaired. The little pieces have not arrived. And there was a wireless from the copper mine. They wish to receive their machinery."

"They'll have to wait until the amphibian's airworthy!" he snapped. "They know that!"

"Si, patron." Maria emerged from a door beneath him, stepped out onto the blue tiles of the courtyard. She was a fat, tubular woman encased in a brown dress the color of damp clay. The dress bound her into ribbed lumps as though she had been moulded by a corrugated culvert pipe. Her face was smooth, round, hook-nosed—topped by coarse black hair parted in the middle and braided in two long strands that hung like tassels across the grey shawl covering her shoulders.

Certain Chimu pottery bore likenesses that could have used Maria as a model. The genes that controlled her facial structure had swallowed Inca and Spaniard alike. The victorious Indian features now graced a woman who enjoyed a considerable reputation as a witch. It bothered Jeb not at all that his cook-maid was the local *bruja*, dispensing herbs and amulets along with her household duties.

Maria glanced up at Jeb, averted her eyes as she glimpsed the red and white shorts poorly covered by his robe.

"Is that all the news?" he asked.

She addressed the sidewall of the courtyard. "No, patron. The mayor wishes to enjoy your presence at a fiesta on the evening of Saturday. The boy brought an invitation. I opened it, of course, to see if it was something important that would require …"

"*Ándale!*"

Her gaze darted toward him, away. "Are you going to marry with the mayor's daughter, patron?"

Jeb grinned. "Maria, you're a nosey old hag!"

She smiled, displaying a glittering row of gold-capped teeth. "The Señorita Constancia is very beautiful, patron. She is a virgin of …"

"A pure mango," agreed Jeb.

Maria pulled her shawl more tightly around her shoulders. "*Patron?*"

Jeb recognized the tone: it normally preceded a request for a day off, for a contribution to improve the church bell tower, for medicine for a sick nephew (because the *bruja* knew the limitations of her own magic).

"What is it?" he asked.

She shrugged. "Patron, last night I saw the spirit of my grandfather. Always, when I have this vision, there is violence, and someone dies." Again she shrugged. "Please be careful today, patron."

The dark eyes took another darting look in his direction and away.

There was suddenly no amusement in Jeb at this manifestation of witchcraft. He felt himself genuinely touched by her concern. There were in this town, he knew, people who paid Maria to have omens interpreted. For one brief moment he even considered telling her about his dream, and then he rejected the idea, half amused at himself.

In the distance, the train from Puerto Bolivar sent its whistle hooting against the hills. Momentarily, all other sounds hung submerged in the echoes. Jeb lifted his attention from the courtyard. Across the red-tiled rooftops he could see the outline of the first cordilleras lifting to the distant Andes and the *Anti-Suyo*: the great "Eastern Jungle" of the Incas. In the middle distance the green hills were split by the notch that spilled the Rio Mavari into the gorge below Milagro. From his balcony, Jeb could just see the edge of the river's upper pool where he kept the little floatplane.

A harpy eagle soared across the near hills, catching up Jeb's mind in the close awareness of flight. The eagle drifted into a thermal, rode away upward like a glider. He watched the bird until it became lost in the misty, heat-wrinkled air.

Maria scuffed her feet on the tiles. "Forgive me, patron, for bothering you with my vision. Do you desire your bath now?"

Jeb snapped his fingers at her. "Yes. And I want *you* to scrub my back!"

The old woman ducked her head to conceal a grin, spoke in a shocked tone: "*Señor!*" She shuffled out of sight below. There came the sound of water splashing into the ten-gallon tin that served Jeb as a shower.

And faintly behind that sound Jeb heard the exhalation of steam—like a tired sigh—from the morning train.

That crazy Bannon dame will probably be on that train, he thought. *Well, she can just go back on the train!*

High-Opp

EMASI! Each Man A Separate Individual!

That is the rallying cry of the Seps, the Separatists engaged in a class war against the upper tiers of a society driven entirely by opinion polls.

Those who score high in the polls, the High-Opps, live in plush apartments, with comfortable jobs, every possible convenience. But those who happen to be low-opped, find themselves crowded in Warrens, with harsh lives and brutal conditions.

Daniel Movius, Ex-Senior Liaitor, rides high in the opinion polls until he becomes a casualty, brushed aside by a very powerful man. Low-opped and abandoned, Movius finds himself fighting for survival in the city's underworld. There, the opinion of the masses is clear: It is time for a revolution against the corrupt super-privileged. And every revolution needs a leader.

Sample Chapter

People averting their faces as they walked past the office door finally wore through his numbness. Daniel Movius began to clench and unclench his fists. He jerked out of his chair, strode to the window, stared at the morning light on the river.

Far out across the river, in silver layers up the Council Hills, he could see the fluting, inverted stalagmites of the High-Opp apartments. And down below them, the drabness, the smoke, the dismal carpet of factories and Warrens.

Back into that? Damn them!

Footsteps. Movius whirled.

A man walked past the door, examined the blank opposite wall of the corridor. Movius raged inwardly. *Sephus! You son of a Sep!* A woman followed. *Bista! I'd as soon make love to a skunk!*

Yet only yesterday she had made courting gestures, bending toward him over her desk to show the curves under the light green coveralls.

He hurled himself into his chair, sent the angry thoughts after them, the words he dared not use. "Avert your faces, you clogs! Don't look at me!"

Another thought intruded. In Roper's name, where was Cecelia? Was she another averted face?

Two men appeared in the doorway pushing a handcart loaded with boxes. Movius did not recognize them, but the LP above their lapel numbers told him. Workers. Labor Pool rabbits. But now he was one of the rabbits. Back into the LP. No more special foods at the restricted restaurants, no more extra credit allowance, no Upper Rank apartment, no car, no driver, no more courting gestures from such as Bista. Today, he was

Daniel Movius, EX-Senior Liaitor.

One of the workmen at the door coughed, looked at the desk plaque which Movius had not yet removed. "Excuse me, sir."

"Yes?" His voice still held its tone of command.

The workman swallowed. "We were told to move the Liaitor files to storage. Is this ...."

He could see the workmen's manner change. "Well, if you'll excuse us, we have work to do." The men came in with an overplayed clatter of officiousness, banging the handcart against the desk. They turned their backs on him, began emptying files into boxes.

Stupid low-opp rabbits!

Movius finished dumping the contents of his desk drawers into the wastebasket, topped the pile with his name plaque. He saved only a sheet of pale red paper. The message chute had disgorged the paper onto his desk less than an hour ago, as he'd been sorting the morning mail.

"Opinion SD22240368523ZX:

"On this date, the Stackman Absolute Sample having been consulted, the governmental function of Liaitor is declared abolished.

"The Question:

"For tax economy reasons, would you favor elimination of the supernumerary department of Liaitor?

"Yes: 79.238 percentum.

"No: .647 percentum.

"Undecided: 20.115 percentum.

"May the Majority rule."

With motions of thinly suppressed violence, Movius folded the paper, thrust it into a pocket. "For tax economy reasons!" They could get a yes-opp matricide for tax economy reasons!

One last look around the office. It was a big place, scaled for a large man, an orderliness to it under the apparently random placement of desk, filing cabinets, piled baskets of papers. There was a smell about the room of oily furniture polish and that kind of bitter chemical odor found in the presence of much paper. It was a room with an air of dedication and no doubt about it. Dedication to quadruplicate copies and *the-right-way-of-doing-the-job*.

Movius noted that his phone had been dislodged from its cradle beside the desk. He replaced it, ran a hand through his stubble of close-cropped sandy hair, unwilling now that the moment had come, to say goodbye to this space in which he had worked four years. The room fitted him like an old saddle or like the body marks in a long-used bed. He had worn his grooves into the place.

Low-opped! And with so much unfinished work. Bu-Opp and Bu-Q were going to be at each others throats before the month was out. The government was damned soon going to find out it had need for Liaison. The bureaus were too jealous of their domains.

Damn them!

He stared at the workmen. They had cleared two files, were emptying a third. Movius was ignored; another discard to be stored away and forgotten. He wanted to fling himself on the men, knock them into a corner, scatter the papers, wreck things, tear things, destroy. He turned and walked quietly out of the office, out of the building.

On the front steps he paused, his eyes seeking out his parking slot in the third row. There was Navvy London, the driver, leaning against the familiar black scarab shape of the car. THE CAR—a primary token of authority. Sunlight shimmered on the flat antenna which spanned the curving roof. Movius looked up to the left where the scintillant red relay ship hovered above the spire of the prime generator, sending out its invisible flagellae of communication and energy beams from which the city sucked its power.

He wished for the strength to hurl all of his pent-up curses at this symbol of authority. Instead, he lowered his eyes, again sought out the car, that tiny extension of the relay ship. Navvy leaned against the grill in his characteristic slouch, reading a book—one of those *inevitably* deep things he *always* carried. The driver pulled at his lower lip with thumb and forefinger, turned a page. Movius suspected that some of Navvy's books were on the contraband lists, but the man was the kind to carry it off. A look of youthful innocence in his brown eyes, a wisp of black hair down across his forehead to heighten the effect. "A contraband book, sir? Great Gallup! I didn't think there were any more of those things drifting about. Thought the government had burned them all. Fellow handed it to me on the street the other day when I asked what he was reading."

Seeing Navvy brought back a disquieting thought: How had Navvy known about the low-opp? How did a Labor Pool driver get official information before it became official?

Movius slipped between the First Rank cars, the Second Rank cars, slowed his pace as he approached the relaxed figure of the driver.

Navvy sensed Movius' presence, looked up, pushed himself away from the car. His young-old face became contemplative. "Now do you believe me, sir?"

Movius drew a deep breath. "How did you know?"

The contemplative look was replaced by casualness. "It came over the LP grapevine."

"That's what you said before. I want to know how."

"Maybe you'll find out now that you're an LP," said Navvy. He turned toward the car. "Anyplace I can take you? They haven't assigned me yet. They're still upstairs wrangling over who'll get my carcass."

"I'm no longer privileged, Navvy. It's forbidden."

"So it's forbidden." He opened the rear door of the car. "They know where they can put their forbiddens. One last ride for old time's sake."

Why not? thought Movius. He shrugged, slipped into the car, felt the solid assurance of the slamming door. Navvy took his place in front.

"Where to, sir?"

"The apartment, I guess."

Navvy flicked the power-receiver switch, turned to back the car from its slot. Movius watched the concentration on the man's face. That was one of Navvy's secrets, a power of concentration, of storing up. But what about the other secret?

"Why won't you tell me *how* you came by the information?"

"You'd only accuse me of being a separatist again."

Movius felt a humorless smile twitch at his lips, remembering their conversation that morning on the way from the apartment. Navvy had said, "Sir, probably I shouldn't be talking, but I've word they're going to low-opp you today."

It had been an ice-water statement, doubly confusing because it came from his driver, someone like an extension of the car.

"Nonsense! Silly scuttlebutt!"

"No, sir. It's over the grapevine. The question was put on the eight o'clock."

Movius glanced at his watch. Ten minutes to nine. They almost always were passing the Bu-Psych Building about this time. He turned. There was the grey stone pile, early workers streaming up the steps.

A question on the eight o'clock? Movius could picture the returns ticking into the computers—Shanghai, Rangoon, Paris, New York, Moscow…. The Comp Section, working at top speed, could have results in two hours. It was impossible that anyone could know the results of an eight o'clock before ten. He explained this fact to Navvy.

"You'll see," said Navvy. "Those autocratic High-Opps have you picked for the long slide down."

And Movius remembered he had chuckled. "The government doesn't function that way, Navvy. Majority opinion rules."

What a trite set of mouthing's those were when he thought back on them. Right out of the approved history books. Right out of the Bureau of Information blathering. But these thoughts brought a sense of uneasiness. He twisted his lapel, looked down at the pale mauve and white of his coveralls, code colors for Tertiary Bureau heads. All of his clothes would have to be dyed. He fingered his identification number on the lapel, the red T stitched above the number. That would be ripped off, LP replacing it.

Labor Pool! Damn them!

Penalty service could scarcely be worse.

The car was climbing through the privileged section now, Gothic canyons of silvery stone interspersed with green parks. There was an air of seclusion and reserved quiet in the privileged sections never found in the bawdy scrambling of the Warrens.

Movius wondered if the word already was out to his apartment manager.

A Game of Authors

In pursuit of a scoop, American journalist Hal Garson follows up on a mysterious, desperate letter that points to the whereabouts of legendary author Antone Luac, who vanished without a trace in Mexico years ago. The celebrated writer's disappearance is an enduring mystery, and Garson senses this story will make his career.

Despite warnings, he travels to isolated Ciudad Brockman and begins asking questions ... too many questions, which place him in the crossfire of a local crime lord, a Communist insurgent group, and finally to the imprisoned writer—and his beautiful daughter—who may not want to be found.

Sample Chapter

Hal Garson, a tall, blond young man with deep-set blue eyes beneath bushy brows, stepped off the Mexican National Railways' train from Guadalajara, plopped his suitcase in the yellow dust.

Ciudad Brockman—here the search really begins, he thought. And then: *The trouble with Antone Luac was that he was too good a cynic. People are of two minds about a successful cynic: they admire his wit, and they fear his attention. A successful cynic can't just disappear. People secretly want him to come to a bad end—and they want the gory details.*

The somber look of Ciudad Brockman caught Garson emotionally. It lay brooding and silent in the siesta-time heat, crouched against a dun-colored mountain like a last stronghold of feudalism held at bay. The mountain formed a threatening backdrop for the city profile of orange roof tiles and jagged steeples.

The look of the place was fitting, all of a piece with the letter from Eduardo Gomez Refugio. The letter had come to Garson in Seattle, forwarded through a magazine that had published a Garson short story about a Mexican *brasero* in the United States.

"Dear Ser: I rid you history in magzine all aboat good Mejicano werk in Unitd Stados. I want much to go Unitd Stados for brazero werk. Now I werk for bad man gangster from Unitd Stados. He is sicret in Ciudad Brockman. He esend meny brazero to Unitd Stados. Never esend mi, Eduardo Gomez Refugio. I giv all history to you ser when you esend mi United Stados for werk brazero. Plis to be very sicret aboat letter to you. He kill mi. You come to Ciudad Brockman and see I spik truth werds. You ask at Tintoreria Nueva York my cousin Lalo. He to tell mi when you say it and nobody lern. For truth my wards I esend letter of gangster to see his fingerprints for F.B.I. of Unitd Stados. Also his name.

Yours affectionately,
Eduardo Gomez Refugio"

Enclosed had been a sheet of bond paper, and on it in a small script a shard of prose—beautifully simple, tantalizing for its incompleteness; a satiric love scene between someone called Elena and someone called Harold. On the back of the sheet was a signature in the same hand: *Antone Cual*—and what looked like a grocery list in Spanish.

The prose and name carried an odd sense of familiarity to Garson. And the letter with its air of conspiracy, its plea for caution and secrecy, made him chuckle.

But there had been something pathetic about the Mexican's plea—a story behind the letter's labored English that told of a struggle to conquer an alien tongue with nothing more than a dictionary and possibly a phrase book.

Garson's atlas showed Ciudad Brockman more than 3,000 miles south of Seattle, deep in the Mexican state of Jalisco. Much too far away for the answering of a plea from a half-illiterate Mexican. The letter and enclosure were touched by mystery, but not worth an expenditure of time by a professional writer whose working hours were mortgaged to previous commitments.

He was on the point of filing the letter under unfinished business—in case he ever *happened* to visit Ciudad Brockman—when his gaze again rested on that neat, concise signature: *Antone Cual.* Garson's eyes made a sudden reversal of direction, and the impact of what he saw brought a tremble to his hand as he bent over the paper.

Cual is a simple anagram on Luac! he thought.

He got out the correct volume of his encyclopedia, found the reference:

"Luac, Antone: born Slagville, Iowa, March 21, 1884. Began newspaper career Chicago, Ill., 1908. Reported Mexican revolution 1912–13 for New York Herald. Went to Europe for Associated Press at start of World War I. Returned January 1919 to career as novelist. His better known works: *A Handbook for Heaven and Hell, Downright Ditties, Choose Your Weapons, The Kaiser's War.* Luac disappeared in Mexico in August, 1932, in company with Anita Peabody, wife of his friend, Alan Peabody, San Francisco drama critic. Peabody later obtained a divorce, naming Luac correspondent. Several attempts to trace the couple have failed. This is considered one of the celebrated disappearances of the Twentieth Century (See also "Famous Missing Persons" by George Powell Davis.)"

Garson found his copy of *A Handbook for Heaven and Hell.* The prose from the mysterious letter carried the same casual, biting simplicity.

The fire of discovery began to burn in Garson. He called his agent in New York, explained about the letter from Mexico. His agent caught some of the same fire. Two days later, Garson had a promise from a national magazine to underwrite part of the expenses for an investigation, or to pay all of the expenses if the story proved true.

That was how he found himself standing beside a railroad track in Mexico, staring moodily at Ciudad Brockman.

His eyes detected a cross on the mountain like a white hole in the blue sky. It prodded his memory of the city's history learned from his quick research. The cross testified to the Latin passion for monuments to human agony. General Brockman's peon legions had held out on that mountain top against ten times their number of Spaniards. Two years of death, torture, and cannon shells for the men on the mountain while the Spanish soldiers lived with the defenders' women in the city.

The mountain and city seemed to say to Garson: "We have seen passion, misery, death and tears before. What is one more story of these things to us?"

A nervous laugh at such dark thoughts escaped Garson. He looked around for a taxi.

Ahead of him a cobbled avenue lined by scarred, dusty trees and high-walled cornfields stretched across the valley floor toward the city and overhanging mountain. The avenue carried traffic of two slow motion burros and a peon. Muddy plaster peeled from the walls lining the avenue, half obliterating the splashed red paint of election announcements.

Over it all, the sun, like a giant ember, seared everything to dusty silence.

To Garson's left under the open shed of the railroad station, Indians sat on benches—men with huaraches on their feet, dirty white trousers, and the hand-embroidered white shirts they wore to market; the shawled women in black or Carmelite brown dresses, like brooding hens, like pieces of the earth. Children played in the dust beside tethered pigs and chickens. Some of the Indians slept with their heads tilted back, faces hidden beneath straw sombreros. Others stared silently at Garson.

They saw the *gringo* cut of his clothes, the harsh jaw line, the air of purpose about him. From these things the cinema-steeped Mexicans built a picture of something secretive and official. Before nightfall they were telling each other that he must really be an American secret agent come to investigate the local mystery: the Hacienda Cual.

There was no sign of a taxi. Garson wondered if he would have to walk the sun-scorched avenue. At every other station in Mexico he had been overwhelmed with offers of service. Here, no one approached him.

Then, a group of Indians standing with their backs to him near a wall at the far corner of the station moved aside. Garson saw the hood of an automobile. He stepped forward to get a better look, and the car moved away from the wall.

It was a black limousine with a wooden box newly roped onto the rear. But Garson's attention remained fixed on the young woman in the rear seat. She had reddish auburn hair, large eyes of a darkness that seemed to trap the light, a complexion like translucent alabaster that—in this latitude—spoke of seclusion, of an old-world custom that hid the fair virgins behind high walls and alert duennas.

As the limousine moved past him, the woman turned, stared directly at Garson. She seemed to catalog him and discard him all in the time that it took her long lashes to flick once over her eyes.

The limousine turned up the avenue, gathered speed. And only then did Garson's mind—assembling the other elements of the scene—tell him that the man beside the driver had worn crossed bandoliers, studded with cartridges, and held a rifle sternly upright.

And Garson thought: *I'd disappear in Mexico myself for something like that!* And for the first time, it occurred to him to ask himself: *Just what did Anita Peabody really look like? Was she as beautiful as that?* The newspaper pictures he had seen—faded and with the woman appearing somehow lumpy in the flapper costume of the era—had left Garson dissatisfied.

A church bell began tolling in the city: a hollow, off-key sound that echoed from the mountain. And now, a pinch-faced boy ran around the station wall, stopped in front of Garson. The marks of Spain and the New World were pressed into the boy's features as though by a sculptor with a heavy thumb.

"*Libre, Señor?*" asked the boy.

"*Libre*" translated to "taxi" in Garson's mind. He said, "*Sí.*"

The boy jerked Garson's suitcase from the ground, led the way at a dog trot through the silently staring Indians. On the opposite side of the station where the limousine had been there was a telephone. Soon, a taxi appeared on the cobbled avenue, bouncing and careening as it sped toward them.

The El Palacio Hotel was a one-story building, tile-floored, dim and cool behind a deep arcade that fronted on a garden plaza. The lobby held three rows of tables that could have been transplanted unchanged from a New York soda parlor, circa 1900. They were marble-topped, set in spindle-legged wrought iron baskets. The chairs had the same unsubstantial twisted-wire appearance.

Two delicatessen cabinets flanked the hotel's registration desk. The glass fronts of the cabinets revealed rows of bottled beer, American process cheeses, and slabs of Spam.

The clerk was a dark-skinned little man with bright hard eyes, a delicate line of mustache, and the hawk beak of a grandee.

He wrote a room number after Garson's signature in the heavy register, said, "*Gabriél Villazana, a sus ordenes, Señor.*"

Garson's mind did its usual slow-motion translation, noting that the clerk had identified himself as Gabriél Villazana.

He gave his *when-in-doubt* answer: "*Gracias.*" The clerk nodded, waved up an urchin who staggered along beneath Garson's bag.

The room was at the end of a hall off the lobby. It was a high-ceilinged space with a half wall in one corner separating shower and toilet. The light came from a skylight directly above a brass spool bed that sagged in the center. There was a mildewed smell about the room. Garson noted that a pile of dead crickets had been swept into one corner.

Gabriél Villazana handed Garson a heavy iron key for the door, accepted his tip with a swift motion of hand into pocket, produced a yellow envelope from another pocket.

"Para usted, Señor."

Garson took the envelope, saw that it was a telegram addressed to him at "El Mejor Hotel de Ciudad Brockman."

The best hotel in the city. He grinned, tore open the envelope. It was from his agent:

"The Times morgue says Anita Peabody secretary-treasurer of Friends of the Poor: on first list of front organizations. Branches in Mexico. Maybe this helps. Maybe it only confuses. Good hunting."

Garson re-read the telegram. *Something to do with the communists in this?* And he thought of the bitter cynicism behind Antone Luac's writing. *Not a chance! Luac was an incipient royalist. He'd spit in the Reds' eyes!*

He tossed the telegram onto the swaybacked bed, decided to use the siesta time for a shower, shave, and change of clothing before seeking out his contact at the *Tintoreria Nueva York*—The New York Dry Cleaners.

It turned out to be a day of half-accomplishments for Garson. And the telegram kept returning to his mind, nagging at him. He wondered if there were a secret message in the telegram—something urgent his agent felt that he must know.

Or why would he send a telegram?

He decided finally that it was the brooding atmosphere of mystery about Ciudad Brockman causing his uneasiness. But he still did not feel satisfied.

The Tintoreria Nueva York was directly across the garden plaza from the hotel. It fronted on another arcade behind a mosaic walk. The *tintoreria* had once been a residence. The patio glimpsed through a half open door behind the long wooden business counter had a cracked fountain, rows of potted plants.

Eduardo Gomez's cousin was a blond, Germanic type—round cheeks, a sunburned complexion, small eyes, a personality like an adding machine. What did not add up to money for this man did not exist. He gained interest only when Garson—with the aid of a phrase book—said that he had *business* with Eduardo Gomez.

Through frequent reference to the phrase book and a pocket dictionary, Garson presently understood that Eduardo Gomez possibly would be in town that day— possibly the next day—possibly the following week—or perhaps not for a month.

Garson turned the conversation to the Hacienda Cual, saw the cousin mentally retreat. A door seemed to close behind his eyes.

A customer entered the *tintoreria*. The cousin excused himself.

Garson returned to the hotel, feeling his uneasiness intensified.

What did Eduardo Gomez write in his letter? "He kill mi." *Could there be something in that?*

Gabriél Villazana, the hotel clerk, was disposed to practice his high school English. He was also less inhibited on the subject of the Hacienda Cual.

"*Sí, Señor.* Un mystery. Very big mystery." He leaned across his registration desk. "The trucks, *Señor.*"

"Trucks? What trucks?"

"Every three, four months, *Señor.* They come. They go."

"What's in them?"

Gabriél Villazana shrugged. "*Quién sabe?*" He cocked his head to one side. "Perhaps you are interested in the *Señorita* Cual, *Señor.*" His eyes rolled heavenward. "Ah, *Señor.* She is a mango!"

It turned out that a "mango" could be literally translated as "a dish." Garson immediately recalled the queenly young woman in the limousine.

The conversation turned to the peace and beauty of Ciudad Brockman. Gabriél Villazana emphasized that there had not been a gun fight in the plaza for almost two years.

Garson registered appropriate admiration, returned to the subject of the Hacienda Cual. "Is it far from here?"

"No, *Señor.* One hour by car." Abruptly, he stared at Garson with a look of shock. "But you are not thinking of going there, *Señor?*"

"Why not?"

"They kill you, *Señor!*"

"Huh?"

Gabriél Villazana became excited, lapsed partly into Spanish with bits of shattered English.

There were guards at the hacienda. Very fierce guards. People disappeared. When one approached the Hacienda Cual there were warning shots—then… Again, the expressive shrug of the shoulders. And the *Señor* Cual, the old man, he had important friends in the government.

Garson tried to get a description of the *Señor* Cual.

It was sufficient for the clerk that the old man of the hacienda had a distinguished face, white hair, and a small beard on the chin that Garson decided must be a goatee.

The incomplete description was another of the afternoon's frustrations.

Garson excused himself.

Gabriél Villazana had one more thought. "Do you have a gun, *Señor?*"

"Of course not. Why do you ask?"

"There are people who do not like those who ask questions about the Hacienda Cual. Perhaps you would like to buy a gun, *Señor*. I know a man who sells them."

"I think not. Thanks anyway."

Again, the shrug of the shoulders.

Garson returned to his room to rest until dinner time. He felt immensely tired, blamed it on the altitude.

Maybe Eduardo Gomez will actually come to town today, he thought.

But he did not really believe it.

"*Señor!* Hssst! *Señor* Garson! Hssst!"

Garson awoke. His eyes looked upward to the skylight of his hotel room. A pale mauve sunset color tinted the opaque glass.

For a moment, he had no idea where he was. Then he remembered: Ciudad Brockman—El Palacio Hotel. He recalled taking a shower in the afternoon heat, deciding to nap before going out to dinner. At the thought of food, his stomach pained him like a child yowling for its supper. He lifted his wristwatch from the bedstand, found that he had been sleeping more than two hours.

What awakened me? Hunger?

Again his stomach constricted.

He could hear a low-voiced conversation in Spanish outside his door. Then "Hsssst! *Señor* Garson!" The voice was high pitched with an air of nervousness.

"Who is it?"

"It is Eduardo Gomez Refugio, *Señor.*"

Garson said, "*Un momento.*" And he thought: *For crying in the dark! He did show today!*

He got up, slipped on a pair of trousers, ran a hand through his hair as he opened the door.

A thin, dark-haired man in a poorly cut navy blue copy of an American business suit stood at the door. The man had eyes like varnished grapes, fearful and subservient. His manner suggested an inner war between servility and self-assertion. He spoke with a grave, comic dignity, a faint bowing of the head.

"*Señor* Garson, I have the honor to be Eduardo Gomez Refugio at your service."

Garson saw Gabriél Villazana, the clerk, behind his caller. The clerk nodded, returned to the front of the hotel. Garson stepped aside.

"Come in. I was just taking a nap."

Eduardo Gomez glanced behind him, entered the room. "*Sí. Sí. Con mucho gusto.*"

Garson closed the door, turned to Gomez. "You speak English, I see."

Gomez stared at him. Then: "Eenglays? Sí, *Señor.* I espeak."

"Well… uh… glad to meet you." Garson held out his hand.

Gomez shook hands with a single, chopping motion. His palm felt hard and calloused. "I esmae, *Señor.*"

Silence settled between them.

Garson felt uncomfortable under the steady examination of the other's eyes.

"I got your letter, Mr. Gomez. And I…"

"*Sí, Señor.* The letter."

Garson had the distinct feeling that Gomez now regretted the letter. There was an air of tragedy about Gomez, a sense of inevitable pathos.

"I'd like to meet this *Señor* Cual," said Garson.

Gomez glanced at his wristwatch. It seemed a motion designed to point out that he owned a watch rather than an actual interest in the time. He returned his attention to Garson.

"You esend me to Uneeted Estados, *Señor?*"

"That's part of the bargain."

The varnished grape eyes looked to the door, back to Garson. "Please not use name of gahngster. Very danger. Many spies. Ciudad Brockman bien full of spies."

"Okay. But can I see this man?"

"I drive automovile of her *señorita* today, *Señor.* Tonight, I come. We espeak."

Garson started to reply, but his memory nudged him to an abrupt silence. He realized that he had seen Eduardo Gomez before, that this thin little man had been sitting behind the wheel of a limousine at the railroad station.

"The *señorita,*" said Garson.

"La hija, Señor."

The daughter! Luac and Anita Peabody have a daughter!

The realization that the daughter was the queenly beauty of the limousine did nothing to reduce Garson's excitement.

"What time will you come?"

Gomez stared at him without comprehension.

He speaks English like I speak Spanish!

Garson gestured to his own wristwatch. "La hora?"

Gomez nodded. "*Sí, Señor. Está la hora.* Tonight I come. You get all history."

"Yes, but…"

"No talk to any mens, *Señor.*" Gomez went to the door, peered out, turned back to Garson. "Very danger."

It dawned on Garson that Gomez was about to leave. The Mexican confirmed this by saying *"Adiós, Señor.* I go with God."

Garson held out a hand. "Wait!"

"*Sí, Señor.* You wait."

With that he was gone, the door closed quickly and softly behind him.

Garson crossed to the door in two steps, opened it, looked out. Most of the lobby tables were occupied. He caught one glimpse of Gomez as the man stepped into the arcade.

I go with God. Such a curious air of tragedy about the statement. Garson experienced a creeping sense of menace, of premonition. He felt that the little man's words might haunt him.

He closed the door, finished dressing.

A warm darkness filled the street outside the arcade when Garson emerged. He stepped from the lobby into a flow of people. There was a new spirit about everyone. Children ran up and down the arcade, whirled around the posts that fronted on the street. Voices were lighter, swifter, as though relieved of some pressure known only to the day.

Ciudad Brockman's mood of sad brooding had disappeared with the coming of night.

"You're the newcomer." It was a deep voice speaking at Garson's shoulder.

He turned, confronted a tall, heavy man with the most ferocious face he had ever seen. The skin was pockmarked, knife-scarred, burnt almost black by the sun. His eyes were like two hunting animals lurking in slitted caves. A wide straw sombrero shaded his face from the arcade's yellow lights, creating an effect of concealment. The man's mouth was a thin slit beneath a handlebar mustache, his chin blunt and square. The nose had been broken and mashed.

"I admit I'm not pretty," said the man, "but it's not polite to stare."

Garson felt his face grow hot. "I'm sorry," he stammered.

"Don't be." The man held out a blunt hand. "I'm Carlos Medina. Call me Choco."

Garson shook hands, felt a casual, almost brutal strength in the other's grip. "I'm Hal Garson."

"Pleased to meet you, Mr. Garson." The English was spoken with easy confidence, totally without a Spanish accent. "What brings you to Ciudad Brockman?"

Garson parried the question. "You sound like someone from the chamber of commerce."

Choco Medina smiled, revealing even, gleaming white teeth. "That's true in a way. I'm an interpreter, and I have a car for hire. I make my living from visitors."

"Not many gringos come here, do they?" asked Garson.

"No, not many."

"You speak excellent English," said Garson.

Medina shrugged. "I was born in El Paso, grew up there and in Juarez."

"Oh." Garson studied the battered face, wondered at the instinctive liking he felt for this man with the evil features. "It just might be that I could use a car and interpreter. What's the rate?"

"Five pesos an hour, twenty-five pesos a day." Again he smiled. "That's for interpreting. The car is one peso a kilometer."

Garson converted twenty-five pesos to dollars at the current exchange: two dollars.

"That's pretty cheap, Mr. Medina."

"In dollars, maybe. But it's the local rate."

"Okay. You're hired."

"When do I start?"

"How about right now?"

"Fine. What are we doing?"

Garson sensed that there was more than casual interest in the question, said, "I'm a writer. I'm here to research the material for a magazine article."

Medina nodded. "Good." He gestured toward the hotel. "Let's get a beer in the lobby here, and you can tell me about it."

Gabriél Villazana served them at one of the marble-topped tables, appeared to focus with an abrupt recognition on Garson's companion.

"*Buenas tardes, Gabriél*," said Medina.

Villazana's head bobbed like a puppet's. "*Buenas tardes, Choco.*" He backed away, turned, almost ran to his counter.

Medina raised his bottle to Garson. "*Salud.*"

"*Salud.*"

The beer tasted cool and tangy. Garson drained half the bottle, put it down, said, "I see you know the clerk."

"We're acquainted."

"He seemed a little afraid of you."

"Maybe I was too rough on him when I asked about my brother." Medina stared at Garson as though expecting a response.

"Am I supposed to say something?" asked Garson. "What about your brother?" He put the beer bottle to his mouth.

"Someone murdered him."

Garson choked on a swallow of beer, coughed. "Sorry." He stared at Medina. "Did Villazana have something to do with it?"

"I don't think so. But he was in Torleon when it happened."

"Torleon?"

"The little town about ten kilometers south of here. It has a good bullring. My brother was murdered on a Sunday—in the crowd coming out of the plaza after the bullfights."

"Who did it?"

Medina leaned back in his chair, shook his head. "I don't know. I wasn't there. I have only one clue—from the daughter of an old man who was hit by a car and killed on the day after my brother was murdered."

Garson wondered why he was being told these things, said, "What's the clue?"

"The nickname of the triggerman. The old man evidently saw only the back of his head, but he heard him called '*La Yegua.*' That's a common nickname for bad-tempered people. It means 'The Mare.'"

"Was the old man killed to shut him up?"

"That's my guess."

"This is very interesting," said Garson. "I'm sorry, of course, to hear about the tragedy in your family."

"Perhaps you can use it in your story, Mr. Garson."

"I doubt it."

"What *are* you going to write about?"

Again Garson sensed that something important hung on his answer. He decided to try for maximum effect. "I'm going to write about Antone Cual. That's not really his name, though. It's Antone *Luac*, the famous writer who disappeared in Mexico in 1932 with another man's wife."

Medina remained impassively calm. "That's a dangerous assignment," he said.

"Why?"

"The hacienda is well guarded."

"Why?"

"Perhaps to keep out such as yourself."

Garson smiled. "He's never been up against me before."

"Do you carry a gun?" asked Medina.

"I won't need a gun." And he thought: *I've never met that question before in my life but here—twice in one day!*

Medina pulled back a flap of his jacket, revealed a heavy revolver in a belt holster. "I carry this for *La Yegua*." He closed his jacket, leaned forward. "Allow me to explain some of our quaint customs. Here in the back country, two out of three people carry a revolver. They are either like me: gunning for someone; or they are afraid someone is gunning for them."

"So?"

"So bodies are occasionally found, Mr. Garson. It is not a rarity. In fact, it is sufficiently common that the police are not too zealous in finding out who pulled the trigger."

"Do the police know you're carrying a gun?"

"Undoubtedly, but they try not to know it officially. No cop wants to buy in on somebody else's feud. This is asking for trouble."

Garson realized abruptly that this was part of the atmosphere that had produced the air of musical comedy melodrama in Eduardo Gomez's letter. He said, "Are you trying to warn me off?"

Medina shrugged. "I merely point out one of the obvious difficulties in your path."

"Thanks. I think I'll go ahead anyway. The American Consulate knows I'm here. Maybe the police would be more zealous in my case."

"We can hope there will be no case, Mr. Garson."

A chill passed over Garson. He reacted with a nervous laugh, said, "I'm just a writer. People don't go around killing writers—*poof!*—just like that!"

"The story going the rounds is that you're a secret agent."

Garson stared at him, shocked. "That's crazy!"

Medina smiled. "Mexicans try to make a mystery out of everything. If there's no mystery, they manufacture one. Sometimes, the mysteries they manufacture are better than real ones."

"But why are they interested in me?"

"Because you've been asking around about the Hacienda Cual—and that's already a favorite mystery here."

"So you already knew why I was here?"

"I've learned not to trust Mexican rumors."

"What are the rumors about the Hacienda Cual?"

"There are so many I wouldn't know where to start."

"Well, it's no mystery, Mr. Medina. It's…"

"Please call me Choco."

"Okay, Choco. The Hacienda Cual is really a very simple matter. It started with a love story—a man and a woman."

Medina raised his eyebrows. "Hell! Everything starts that way!"

Garson laughed, glanced at his wristwatch, was surprised to find it almost seven o'clock.

"Are you expecting someone?" asked Medina.

"No. I'm going to eat dinner and knock off for the night. I can't seem to get enough sleep."

"It's the altitude. You'll get used to it."

"Unless I'm forced to get used to a much higher altitude first."

This seemed to strike Medina as funnier than Garson had expected. The Mexican guffawed, attracting the attention of people at surrounding tables.

"Maybe you don't think writers should go to heaven," said Garson.

Medina wiped a tear from his right eye. "You should write humor, Mr. Garson."

"Perhaps I should."

The Mexican sobered, leaned far back in his chair. "What time will you want me in the morning?"

"Will eight o'clock be all right?"

"Good enough." Medina pushed away from the table, got to his feet. "Then, if you won't be needing me anymore tonight..."

"See you in the morning," said Garson.

Gabriél Villazana came to Garson's table as soon as Choco Medina was gone. "That is a very bad man," said Villazana.

"I suppose so," said Garson. "But I kind of like him."

Villazana's shrug seemed to say that he had done what he could, that all gringos were crazy anyway, that after all only a confirmed idiot stands in the path of fate.

Other WordFire Press Titles by Frank Herbert

Angels' Fall
Destination Void
Direct Descent
A Game of Authors
The Godmakers
High-Opp
Soul Catcher
A Thorn in the Bush

with Bill Ransom

The Jesus Incident
The Lazarus Effect
The Ascension Factor

Our list of other WordFire Press authors and titles is always growing. To find out more and to see our selection of titles, visit us at:

wordfirepress.com

www.ingramcontent.com/pod-product-compliance
Lightning Source LLC
Chambersburg PA
CBHW030412120726
47904CB00007B/2244